THE BOOK-LOVER

A Guide to the Best Reading

BY

JAMES BALDWIN

A Fore Word.

The titlepage of this book explains its plan and purpose. The Courses of Reading and the Schemes for Practical Study, herein indicated, are the outgrowth of the Author's long experience as a lover of books and director of reading. They have been tested and found to be all that is claimed for them. As to the large number of quotations in the first part of the book, they are given in the belief that "in a multitude of counsels there is wisdom." And the Author finds consolation and encouragement in the following words of Emerson: "We are as much informed of a writer's genius by what he selects, as by what he originates. We read the quotation with his eyes, and find a new and fervent sense." As the value of the most useful inventions depends upon thevi ingenious placing of their parts, so the originality of this work may be found to lie chiefly in its arrangement. Yet the writer confidently believes that his readers will enjoy that which he has borrowed, and possibly find aid and encouragement in that which he claims as his own; and therefore this book is sent out with the hope that book-lovers will find in it a safe Guide to the Best Reading.

PRELUDE.

In Praise of Books.

LET us consider how great a commodity of doctrine exists in Books; how easily, how secretly, how safely they expose the nakedness of human ignorance without putting it to shame. These are the masters who instruct us without rods and ferules, without hard words and anger, without clothes or money. If you approach them, they are not asleep; if investigating you interrogate them, they conceal nothing; if you mistake them, they never grumble; if you are ignorant, they cannot laugh at you.

You only, O Books, are liberal and independent. You give to all who ask, and enfranchise all who serve you assiduously. Truly, you are the ears filled with most palatable grains. You are golden urns in which10 manna is laid up; rocks flowing with honey, or rather, indeed, honeycombs; udders most copiously yielding the milk of life; store-rooms ever full; the four-streamed river of Paradise, where the human mind is fed, and the arid intellect moistened and watered; fruitful olives; vines of Engaddi; fig-trees knowing no sterility; burning lamps to be ever held in the hand.

The library, therefore, of wisdom is more precious than all riches; and nothing that can be wished for is worthy to be compared with it. Whosoever acknowledges himself to be a zealous follower of truth, of happiness, of wisdom, of science, or even of the faith, must of necessity make himself a Lover of Books.

RICHARD DE BURY, 1344.

Books are friends whose society is extremely agreeable to me; they are of all ages, and of every country. They have distinguished themselves both in the cabinet and in the field, and obtained high honors for their knowledge of the sciences. It is easy to gain access to them; for they are always at my service, and I admit them to my company, and dismiss them from it, whenever I please. They are never troublesome, but immediately answer every question I ask them. Some relate to me the events of past ages, while11 others reveal to me the secrets of Nature. Some teach me how to live, and others how to die. Some, by their vivacity, drive away my cares and exhilarate my spirits; while others give fortitude to my mind, and teach me the important lesson how to restrain my desires, and to depend wholly on myself. They open to me, in short, the various avenues of all the arts and sciences, and upon their information I safely rely in all emergencies. In return for all these services, they only ask me to accommodate them with a convenient chamber in some corner of my humble habitation, where they may repose in peace; for these friends are more delighted by the tranquility of retirement, than with the tumults of society.

FRANCESCO PETRARCA.

Books are the Glasse of Counsell to dress ourselves by. They are Life's best Business: Vocation to them hath more Emolument coming in, than all the other busie Termes of Life. They are Feelesse Counsellours, no delaying Patrons, of easie Accesse, and kind Expedition, never sending away any Client or Petitioner. They are for Company, the best Friends; in doubts, Counsellours; in Damp, Comforters; Time's Perspective; the home Traveller's Ship, or Horse; the busie Man's best Recreation; the Opiate of idle12 Wearinesse; the Mind's best Ordinary; Nature's Garden and Seed-plot of Immortality.

A WRITER OF THE SIXTEENTH CENTURY (quoted in "Allibone's Dictionary").

But how can I live here without my books? I really seem to myself crippled and only half myself; for if, as the great Orator used to say, arms are a soldier's members, surely books are the limbs of scholars. Corasius says: "Of a truth, he who would deprive me of books, my old friends, would take away all the delight of my life; nay, I will even say, all desire of living."

BALTHASAR BONIFACIUS RHODIGINUS, 1656.

For books are not absolutely dead things, but do contain a potency of life in them to be as active as that soul was whose progeny they are; nay, they do preserve, as in a vial, the purest efficacy and extraction of that living intellect that bred them. I know they are as lively and as vigorously productive as those fabulous dragon's teeth, and, being sown up and down, may chance to spring up armed men.... Many a man lives, a burden to the earth; but a good book is the precious life-blood of a master spirit, embalmed and treasured up on purpose for a life beyond life.

JOHN MILTON.

13

Books are a guide in youth, and an entertainment for age. They support us under solitude, and keep us from being a burden to ourselves. They help us to forget the crossness of men and things, compose our cares and our passions, and lay our disappointments asleep. When we are weary of the living, we may repair to the dead, who have nothing of peevishness, pride, or design in their conversation.

JEREMY COLLIER.

God be thanked for books! They are the voices of the distant and the dead, and make us heirs of the spiritual life of past ages. Books are the true levellers. They give to all who will faithfully use them, the society, the spiritual presence, of the best and greatest of our race. No matter how poor I am; no matter though the prosperous of my own time will not enter my obscure dwelling; if the sacred writers will enter and take up their abode under my roof,—if Milton will cross my threshold to sing to me of Paradise; and Shakspeare to open to me the worlds of imagination and the workings of the human heart; and Franklin to enrich me with his practical wisdom,—I shall not pine for want of intellectual companionship, and I may become a cultivated man, though excluded14 from what is called the best society in the place where I live.

WILLIAM ELLERY CHANNING.

In a corner of my house I have books,—the miracle of all my possessions, more wonderful than the wishing-cap of the Arabian tales; for they transport me instantly, not only to all places, but to all times. By my books I can conjure up before me to a momentary existence many of the great and good men of past ages, and for my individual satisfaction they seem to act again the most renowned of their achievements; the orators declaim for me, the historians recite, the poets sing.

DR. ARNOTT.

Wondrous, indeed, is the virtue of a true book! Not like a dead city of stones, yearly crumbling, yearly needing repair; more like a tilled field, but then a spiritual field; like a spiritual tree, let me rather say, it stands from year to year and from age to age (we have books that already number some hundred and fifty human ages); and yearly comes its new produce of leaves (commentaries, deductions, philosophical, political systems; or were it only sermons, pamphlets, journalistic essays), every one of which is talismanic and thaumaturgic, for it can persuade man. O thou who art able to write a book, which once in two centuries or oftener15 there is a man gifted to do, envy not him whom they name city-builder, and inexpressibly pity him whom they name conqueror or city-burner! Thou, too, art a conqueror and victor; but of the true sort, namely, over the Devil. Thou, too, hast built what will outlast all marble and metal, and be a wonder-bringing city of mind, a temple and seminary and prophetic mount, whereto all kindreds of the earth will pilgrim.

THOMAS CARLYLE.

Good books, like good friends, are few and chosen; the more select, the more enjoyable; and like these are approached with diffidence, nor sought too familiarly nor too often, having the precedence only when friends tire. The most mannerly of companions, accessible at all times, in all moods, they frankly declare the author's mind, without giving offence. Like living friends, they too have their voice and physiognomies, and their company is prized as old acquaintances. We seek them in our need of counsel or of amusement, without impertinence or apology, sure of having our claims allowed. A good book justifies our theory of personal supremacy, keeping this fresh in the memory and perennial. What were days without such fellowship? We were alone in the world without it.

A. BRONSON ALCOTT.

16

Consider what you have in the smallest chosen library. A company of the wisest and wittiest men that could be picked out of all civil countries, in a thousand years, have set in best order the results of their learning and wisdom. The men themselves were hid and inaccessible, solitary, impatient of interruption, fenced by etiquette; but the thought which they did not uncover to their bosom friend is here written out in transparent words to us, the strangers of another age. We owe to books those general benefits which come from high intellectual action. Thus, I think, we often owe to them the perception of immortality. They impart sympathetic activity to the moral power. Go with mean people, and you think life is mean. Then read Plutarch, and the world is a proud place, peopled with men of positive quality, with heroes and demi-gods standing around us, who will not let us sleep. Then they address the imagination: only poetry inspires poetry. They become the organic culture of the time. College education is the reading of certain books which the common sense of all scholars agrees will represent the science already accumulated.... In the highest civilization the book is still the highest delight.

RALPH WALDO EMERSON.

17

A great book that comes from a great thinker,—it is a ship of thought, deep-freighted with truth, with beauty too. It sails the ocean, driven by the winds of heaven, breaking the level sea of life into beauty where it goes, leaving behind it a train of sparkling loveliness, widening as the ship goes on. And what a treasure it brings to every land, scattering the seeds of truth, justice, love, and piety, to bless the world in ages yet to come!

THEODORE PARKER.

What is a great love of books? It is something like a personal introduction to the great and good men of all past times. Books, it is true, are silent as you see them on their shelves; but, silent as they are, when I enter a library I feel as if almost the dead were present, and I know if I put questions to these books they will answer me with all the faithfulness and fulness which has been left in them by the great men who have left the books with us.

JOHN BRIGHT.

I love my books as drinkers love their wine;
The more I drink, the more they seem divine;
With joy elate my soul in love runs o'er,
And each fresh draught is sweeter than before!
Books bring me friends where'er on earth I be,—
Solace of solitude, bonds of society.

I love my books! they are companions dear,
Sterling in worth, in friendship most sincere;18
Here talk I with the wise in ages gone,
And with the nobly gifted in our own:
If love, joy, laughter, sorrow please my mind,
Love, joy, grief, laughter in my books I find.
FRANCIS BENNOCH.
Books are the windows through which the soul looks out.

HENRY WARD BEECHER.

Books are our household gods; and we cannot prize them too highly. They are the only gods in all the mythologies that are beautiful and unchangeable; for they betray no man, and love their lovers. I confess myself an idolater of this literary religion, and am grateful for the blessed ministry of books. It is a kind of heathenism which needs no missionary funds, no Bible even, to abolish it; for the Bible itself caps the peak of this new Olympus, and crowns it with sublimity and glory. Amongst the many things we have to be thankful for, as the result of modern discoveries, surely this of printed books is the highest of all; and I, for one, am so sensible of its merits that I never think of the name of Gutenberg without feelings of veneration and homage.

JANUARY SEARLE.

The only true equalizers in the world are books; the only treasure-house open to all comers is a library; the only wealth which19 will not decay is knowledge; the only jewel which you can carry beyond the grave is wisdom. To live in this equality, to share in these treasures, to possess this wealth, and to secure this jewel may be the happy lot of every one. All that is needed for the acquisition of these inestimable treasures is the love of books.

J. A. LANGFORD.

Let us thank God for books. When I consider what some books have done for the world, and what they are doing; how they keep up our hope, awaken new courage and faith, soothe pain, give an ideal life to those whose homes are hard and cold, bind together distant ages and foreign lands, create new worlds of beauty, bring down truths from heaven,—I give eternal blessings for this gift, and pray that we may use it aright, and abuse it not.

JAMES FREEMAN CLARKE.

Books, we know, Are a substantial world, both pure and good; Round these, with tendrils strong as flesh and blood, Our pastime and our happiness will grow.

WILLIAM WORDSWORTH.

Precious and priceless are the blessings which books scatter around our daily paths. We walk, in imagination, with the noblest20 spirits, through the most sublime and enchanting regions,—regions which, to all that is lovely in the forms and colors of earth,

"Add the gleam,
The light that never was on sea or land,
The consecration and the poet's dream."

A motion of the hand brings all Arcadia to sight. The war of Troy can, at our bidding, rage in the narrowest chamber. Without stirring from our firesides, we may roam to the most remote regions of the earth, or soar into realms where Spenser's shapes of unearthly beauty flock to meet us, where Milton's angels peal in our ears the choral hymns of Paradise. Science, art, literature, philosophy,—all that man has thought, all that man has done,—the experience that has been bought with the sufferings of a hundred generations,—all are garnered up for us in the world of books. There, among realities, in a "substantial world," we move with the crowned kings of thought. There our minds have a free range, our hearts a free utterance. Reason is confined within none of the partitions which trammel it in life. In that world, no divinity hedges a king, no accident of rank or fashion ennobles a dunce or shields a knave. We can select our companions from among the most richly gifted of the sons of God;21 and they are companions who will not desert us in poverty, or sickness, or disgrace.

EDWIN P. WHIPPLE.

My latest passion shall be for books.

FRIEDRICH II. OF PRUSSIA.

For what a world of books offers itself, in all subjects, arts, and sciences, to the sweet content and capacity of the reader? In arithmetic, geometry, perspective, optics, astronomy, architecture, *sculptura, pictura*, of which so many and such elaborate treatises are of late written; in mechanics and their mysteries, military matters, navigation, riding of horses, fencing, swimming, gardening, planting, etc.... What so sure, what so pleasant? What vast tomes are extant in law, physic, and divinity, for profit, pleasure, practice, speculation, in verse or prose! Their names alone are the subject of whole volumes; we have thousands of authors of all sorts, many great libraries, full well furnished, like so many dishes of meat, served out for several palates, and he is a very block that is affected with none of them.

ROBERT BURTON.

Except a living man, there is nothing more wonderful than a book!—a message to us from the dead,—from human souls whom we never saw, who lived perhaps thousands of22 miles away; and yet these, on those little sheets of paper, speak to us, amuse us, vivify us, teach us, comfort us, open their hearts to us as brothers. We ought to reverence books, to look at them as useful and mighty things. If they are good and true, ... they are the message of Christ, the maker of all things, the teacher of all truth.

CHARLES KINGSLEY.

Golden volumes! richest treasures!
Objects of delicious pleasures!
You my eyes rejoicing please,
You my hands in rapture seize.
Brilliant wits and musing sages,
Lights who beamed through many ages,
Left to your conscious leaves their story,
And dared to trust you with their glory;

And now their hope of fame achieved,
Dear volumes!—you have not deceived.
HENRY RANTZAU.

23

CHAPTER I.

On the Choice of Books.

THE choice of books is not the least part of the duty of a scholar. If he would become a man, and worthy to deal with manlike things, he must read only the bravest and noblest books,—books forged at the heart and fashioned by the intellect of a godlike man.—JANUARY SEARLE.

HE most important question for you to ask yourself, be you teacher or scholar, is this: What books shall I read? For him who has inclination to read, there is no dearth of reading matter, and it is obtainable almost for the asking. Books are in a manner thrust upon you almost daily. Shall you read without discrimination whatever comes most readily to hand? As well say that you will accept as a friend and companion every man whom you meet on the street. Shall you read even every good book that comes in your way,24 simply because it is harmless and interesting? It is not every harmless book, nor indeed every good book, that will make your mind the richer for the reading of it. Never, perhaps, has the right choice of books been more difficult than at present; and never did it behoove more strongly both teachers and scholars to look well to the character of that which they read.

First, then, let us consider what books we are to avoid. All will agree that those which are really and absolutely bad should be shunned as we shun a pestilence. In these last years of the nineteenth century there is no more prolific cause of evil than bad books. There are many books so utterly vile that there is no mistaking their character, and no question as to whether they should be avoided. There are others which are a thousand-fold more dangerous because they come to us disguised,—"wolves in sheep's clothing,"—affecting a character of harmlessness, if not of sanctity. I have heard those who ought to know better, laugh at the silly jokes of a very silly book, and offer by way of excuse that there was nothing *very* bad in it. I have heard teachers recommend to their pupils reading matter which, to say the least, was of25 a very doubtful character. Now, the only excuse that can be offered in such cases is ignorance,—"I didn't know there was any harm in the book." But the teacher who through ignorance poisons the moral character and checks the mental growth of his pupils is as guilty of criminal carelessness as the druggist's clerk who by mistake sells arsenic for quinine. Step down and out of that responsible position which you are in no wise qualified to fill! The direction of the pupils' habits of reading, the choice of reading matter for them, is by no means the least of the teacher's duties.

The elder Pliny, eighteen hundred years ago, was accustomed to say that no book was so bad but that some part of it might be read with profit. This may have been true in Pliny's time; but it is very far from correct now-a-days. A large number of books, and many which attain an immense circulation, are but the embodiment of evil from beginning to end; others, although not absolutely and aggressively bad, contain not a single line that can be read with profit.

What are the sure criterions of a bad book? There is no better authority on this subject than the Rev. Robert Collyer. He says: "If26 when I read a book about God, I find that it has put Him farther from me; or about man, that it has put me farther from him; or about this universe, that it has shaken down upon it a new look of desolation, turning a green field into a wild moor; or about life, that it has made it seem a little less worth living, on all accounts, than it was; or about moral principles, that they are not quite so clear and strong as they were when this author began to talk;—then I know that on any of these five cardinal things in the life of man,—his relations to God, to his fellows, to the world about him, and the world within him, and the great principles on which all things stable centre,—*that*, for me, is a bad book. It may chime in with some lurking appetite in my own nature, and so seem to be as sweet as honey to my taste; but it comes to bitter, bad results. It may be food for another; I can say nothing to that. He may be a pine while I am a palm. I only know this, that in these great first things, if the book I read shall touch them at all, it shall touch them to my profit or I will not read it. Right and wrong shall grow more clear; life in and about me more divine; I shall come nearer to my fellows, and God nearer to me, or the thing is a poi27son. Faust, or Calvin, or Carlyle, if any one of these cardinal things is the grain and the grist of the book, and that is what it comes to when I read it, I am being drugged and poisoned; and the sooner I know it the better. I want bread, and meat, and milk, not brandy, or opium, or hasheesh."[1]

And Robert Southey, the poet, expresses nearly the same thing: "Young readers,—you whose hearts are open, whose understandings are not yet hardened, and whose feelings are not yet exhausted nor encrusted with the world,—take from me a better rule than any professors of criticism will teach you! Would you know whether the tendency of a book is good or evil, examine in what state of mind you lay it down. Has it induced you to suspect that what you have been accustomed to think unlawful may after all be innocent, and that may be harmless which you have hitherto been taught to think dangerous? Has it tended to make you dissatisfied and impatient under the control of others, and disposed you to relax in that self-government without which both the laws of God and man tell us there can be no virtue, and, consequently, no happiness? Has it attempted to 28abate your admiration and reverence for what is great and good, and to diminish in you the love of your country and your fellow-creatures? Has it addressed itself to your pride, your vanity, your selfishness, or any other of your evil propensities? Has it defiled the imagination with what is loathsome, and shocked the heart with what is monstrous? Has it disturbed the sense of right and wrong which the Creator has implanted in the human soul? If so, if you are conscious of any or all of these effects, or if, having escaped from all, you have felt that such were the effects it was intended to produce, throw the book in the fire, whatever name it may bear in the titlepage! Throw it in the fire, young man, though it should have been the gift of a friend; young lady, away with the whole set, though it should be the prominent furniture of a rosewood bookcase."[2]

"It is the case with literature as with life," says Arthur Schopenhauer, the German philosopher. "Wherever we turn we come upon the incorrigible mob of humankind, whose name is Legion, swarming everywhere, damaging everything, as flies in summer. Hence the multiplicity of bad books, those exuberant 29weeds of literature which choke the true corn. Such books rob the public of time, money, and attention, which ought properly to belong to good literature and noble aims; and they are written with a view merely to make money or occupation. They are therefore not merely useless, but injurious. Nine tenths of our current literature has no other end but to inveigle a thaler or two out of the public pocket, for which purpose author, publisher, and printer are leagued together.... Of bad books we can never read too little; of the good, never too much. The bad are intellectual poison, and undermine the understanding."[3]

From Thomas Carlyle's inaugural address at Edinburgh on the occasion of his installation as rector of the University in 1866, I quote the following potent passage: "I do not know whether it has been sufficiently brought home to you that there are two kinds of books. When a man is reading on any kind of subject, in most departments of books,—in all books, if you take it in a wide sense,—he will find that there is a division into good books and bad books: everywhere a good kind of a book 30and a bad kind of a book. I am not to assume that you are unacquainted or ill-acquainted with this plain fact; but I may remind you that it is becoming a very important consideration in our day.... There is a number, a frightfully increasing number, of books that are decidedly, to the readers of them, not useful. But an ingenious reader will learn, also, that a certain number of books were written by a supremely noble kind of people; not a very great number of books, but still a number fit to occupy all your reading industry, do adhere more or less to that side of things. In short, as I have written it down somewhere else, I conceive that books are like men's souls, divided into sheep and goats. Some few are going up, and carrying us up, heavenward; calculated, I mean, to be of priceless advantage in teaching,—in forwarding the teaching of all generations. Others, a frightful multitude, are going down, down; doing ever the more and the wider and the wilder mischief. Keep a strict eye on that latter class of books, my young friends!"

Speaking of those books whose inward character and influence it is hard at first to discern, John Ruskin says: "Avoid especially that class of literature which has a knowing31 tone; it is the most poisonous of all. Every good book, or piece of book, is full of admiration and awe: it may contain firm assertion or stern satire, but it never sneers coldly, nor asserts haughtily; and it always leads you to reverence or love something with your whole heart. It is not always easy to distinguish the satire of the venomous race of books from the satire of the noble and pure ones; but, in general, you may notice that the cold-blooded Crustacean and Batrachian books will sneer at sentiment, and the warm-blooded, human books at sin.... Much of the literature of the present day, though good to be read by persons of ripe age, has a tendency to agitate rather than confirm, and leaves its readers too frequently in a helpless or hopeless indignation, the worst possible state into which the mind of youth can be thrown. It may, indeed, become necessary for you, as you advance in life, to set your hand to things that need to be altered in the world, or apply your heart chiefly to what must be pitied in it, or condemned; but for a young person the safest temper is one of reverence, and the safest place one of obscurity. Certainly at present, and perhaps through all your life, your teachers are wisest when they make you32 content in quiet virtue; and that literature and art are best for you which point out, in common life and familiar things, the objects for hopeful labor and for humble love."[4]

There would be fewer bad books in the world if readers were properly informed and warned of their character; and we may believe that the really vicious books would soon cease to exist if their makers and publishers were popularly regarded with the same detestation as other corrupters of the public morals. "He who has published an injurious book," says Robert South, "sins, as it were in his very grave; corrupts others while he is rotting himself." Addison says much the same thing: "Writers of great talents, who employ their parts in propagating immorality, and seasoning vicious sentiments with wit and humor, are to be looked upon as the pests of society and the enemies of mankind. They leave books behind them to scatter infection and destroy their posterity. They act the counterparts of a Confucius or a Socrates, and seem to have been sent into the world to deprave human nature, and sink it into the condition of brutality."[5]

33

And William Cobbett is still more severe in his denunciation. In his "Advice to Young Men," he says: "I hope that your taste will keep you aloof from the writings of those detestable villains who employ the powers of their mind in debauching the minds of others, or in endeavors to do it. They present their poison in such captivating forms that it requires great virtue and resolution to withstand their temptations; and they have, perhaps, done a thousand times as much mischief in the world as all the infidels and atheists put together. These men ought to be held in universal abhorrence, and never spoken of but with execration."

But the shunning of bad books is only one of the problems presented to us in the choice of our reading. In the great multitude of really good and valuable books, how shall we choose those which are of the most vital importance to us to know? The universal habit of desultory reading—reading simply to be entertained—is a habit not to be indulged in, nor encouraged, by scholars or by those who aspire to the station of teachers. There are perhaps a score of books which should be read and studied by every one who claims the title of reader; but, aside from these, each34 person should determine, through a process of rigid self-examination, what course of reading and what books are likely to produce the most profitable results to him. Find out, if possible, what is your special bent of mind. What line of inquiry or investigation is the most congenial to your taste or mental capacity? Having determined this question, let your reading all centre upon that topic of study which you have made your own,—let it be Literature, Science, History, Art, or any of the innumerable subdivisions of these subjects. In other words, choose a specialty, and follow it with an eye single to it alone.

Says Frederic Harrison: "Every book that we take up without a purpose is an opportunity lost of taking up a book with a purpose; every bit of stray information which we cram into our heads without any sense of its importance is for the most part a bit of the most useful information driven out of our heads and choked off from our minds.... We know that books differ in value as much as diamonds differ from the sand on the sea-shore, as much as our living friend differs from a dead rat. We know that much in the myriad-peopled world of books—very much in all kinds—is trivial, enervating, inane, even35 noxious. And thus, where we have infinite opportunities of wasting our effort to no end, of fatiguing our minds without enriching them, of clogging the spirit without satisfying it, there, I cannot but think, the very infinity of opportunities is robbing us of the actual power of using them.... To know anything that turns up is, in the infinity of knowledge, to know nothing. To read the first book we come across, in the wilderness of books, is to learn nothing. To turn over the pages of ten thousand volumes is to be practically indifferent to all that is good."[6]

"It is of paramount importance," says Schopenhauer, "to acquire the art*not* to read; in other words, of not reading such books as occupy the public mind, or even those which make a noise in the world, and reach several editions in their first and last year of existence. We should recollect that he who writes for fools finds an enormous audience, and we should devote the ever scant leisure of our circumscribed existence to the master-spirits of all ages and nations, those who tower over humanity, and whom the voice of Fame proclaims: only such writers cultivate and instruct us."[7]

36

And John Ruskin offers the following pertinent advice to beginners: "It is of the greatest importance to you, not only for art's sake, but for all kinds of sake, in these days of book deluge, to keep out of the salt swamps of literature, and live on a little rocky island of your own, with a spring and a lake in it, pure and good. I cannot, of course, suggest the choice of your library to you, for every several mind needs different books; but there are some books which we all need, and assuredly, if you read Homer, Plato, Æschylus, Herodotus, Dante, Shakspeare, and Spenser as much as you ought, you will not require wide enlargement of your shelves to right and left of them for purposes of perpetual study. Among modern books, avoid generally magazine and review literature. Sometimes it may contain a useful abridgment or a wholesome piece of criticism; but the chances are ten to one it will either waste your time or mislead you. If you want to understand any subject whatever, read the best book upon it you can hear of; not a review of the book.... A common book will often give you much amusement, but it is only a noble book which will give you dear friends."

37

If any of us could recall the time which we have spent in desultory and profitless reading, and devote it now faithfully to the prosecution of that special line of study which ought, long ago, to have been chosen, how largely we might add to our fund of useful knowledge, and how grandly we might increase our intellectual stature! "And again," remarks James Herbert Morse, "if I could recover the hours idly given to the newspaper, not for my own gratification, but solely for my neighbor at the breakfast-table, I could compass a solid course of English and American history, get at the antecedents of political parties in the two countries, and give the reasons for the existence of Gladstone and Parnell, of Blaine and Edmunds, in modern politics—and there is undoubtedly a reason for them all. Two columns a day in the newspapers—which I could easily have spared, for they were given mainly to murder-trials and the search for corpses, or to the romance of the reporter concerning the same—have during the last ten years absorbed just about the time I might have spent in reading a very respectable course in history,—one embracing, say, Curtius and Grote for Greece, Mommsen, Merivale, and Gibbon for Rome, Macaulay38 and Green for my roots in Saxondom, Bancroft, Hildreth, and Palfrey for the ancestral tree in America, together with a very notable excursion into Spain and Holland with Motley and Prescott,—a course which I consider very desirable, and one which should set up a man of middle age very fairly in historical knowledge. I am sure I could have saved this amount out of any ten years of my newspaper reading alone, without cutting off any portion of that really valuable contribution for which the daily paper is to be honored, and which would be needed to make me an intelligent man in the history of my own times."[8]

It is not necessary that, in selecting a library or in choosing what you will read, you should have many books at your disposal. A few books, well chosen and carefully read, will be of infinitely more value to you than any miscellaneous collection, however large. It is possible for "the man of one book" to be better equipped in knowledge and literary attainments than he whose shelves are loaded with all the fashionable literature of the day. If your means will not permit you the luxury of a library, buy one book, or a few books, chosen with special reference to the line of 39reading which you have determined upon. Let no honey-mouthed book-agent persuade you to buy of his wares, unless they bear exactly upon your specialty. You cannot afford to waste money on mere catchpenny or machine publications, whose only recommendation is that they are harmless and that they sell well. That man is to be envied who can say, "I have a library of fifty or of a hundred volumes, all relating to my chosen line of thought, and not a single inferior or worthless volume among them."

I have before me a list of books,—"books fashioned by the intellect of godlike men,"—books which every person who aspires to the rank of teacher or scholar should regard as his inheritance from the master-minds of the ages. If you know these books—or some of them—you know much of that which is best in the great world of letters. You cannot afford to live in ignorance of them.

Plato's Dialogues (Jowett's translation).
The Orations of Demosthenes on the Crown.
Bacon's Essays.
Burke's Orations and Political Essays.
Macaulay's Essays.
Carlyle's Essays.
[40]Webster's Select Speeches.
Emerson's Essays.
The Essays of Elia, by Charles Lamb.
Ivanhoe, by Sir Walter Scott.
David Copperfield, by Charles Dickens.
Vanity Fair, by William Makepeace Thackeray.
Hypatia, by Charles Kingsley.
The Mill on the Floss, by George Eliot.
The Marble Faun, by Nathaniel Hawthorne.
The Sketch Book, by Washington Irving.
Les Miserables, by Victor Hugo.
Wilhelm Meister, by Goethe (Carlyle's trans.).
Don Quixote, by Cervantes.
Homer's Iliad (Derby's or Chapman's translation).
Homer's Odyssey (Bryant's translation).
Dante's Divina Commedia (Longfellow's trans.).
Milton's Paradise Lost.
Shakspeare's Works.
Mrs. Browning's Poems.
Longfellow's Poetical Works.
Goethe's Faust (Bayard Taylor's translation).

I have named but twenty-five authors; but each of these, in his own line of thought and endeavor, stands first in the long roll of immortals. When you have the opportunity to make the acquaintance of such as these, will you waste your time with writers whom you would be ashamed to number among your personal friends? "Will you go and gossip with your housemaid or your stable boy, when you may talk with kings and queens, while this eternal court is open to you, with its society wide as the world, multitudinous[41] as its days, the chosen, the mighty, of every place and time? Into that you may enter always; in that you may take fellowship and rank according to your wish; from that, once entered into it, you can never be outcast but by your own fault; by your aristocracy of companionship there, your inherent aristocracy will be assuredly tested, and the motives with which you strive to take high place in the society of the living, measured, as to all the truth and sincerity that are in them, by the place you desire to take in this company of the dead."[2]

CHAPTER II.

How to Read.

AND as for me, though I con but lite,
On bookes for to rede I me delite,
And to hem yeve I faith and credence,
And in my herte have hem in reverence
So hertely, that there is game none,
That from my bookes maketh me to gone,
But it be seldome on the holy daie,
Save certainly, whan that the month of May
Is comen, and that I heare the foules sing,
And that the floures ginnan for to spring,
Farwell my booke, and my devotion.
GEOFFREY CHAUCER.

AVING chosen the books which are to be our friends and counsellors, the next question to be considered is, How shall we use them? Shall we read them through as hastily as possible, believing that the more we read, the more learned we are? Or shall we not derive more profit by reading slowly, and by making the subject-matter of each book *thoroughly our own*? I do not believe that any general rule43 can be given with reference to this matter. Some readers will take in a page at a glance, and will more thoroughly master a book in a week than others could possibly master it in six months. It required Frederick W. Robertson half a year to read a small manual of chemistry, and thoroughly to digest its contents. Miss Martineau and Auguste Comte were remarkably slow readers; but then, that which they read "lay fructifying, and came out a living tree with leaves and fruit." Yet it does not follow that the same rule should apply to readers of every grade of genius.

It is generally better to read by subjects, to learn what different writers have thought and said concerning that matter of which you are making a special study. Not many books are to be read hastily through. "A person who was a very great reader and hard thinker," says Bishop Thirlwall, "once told me that he never took up a book except with the view of making himself master of some subject which he was studying, and that while he was so engaged he made all his reading converge to that point. In this way he might read parts of many books, but not a single one from 'end to end.' This I take to be an excellent method of study, but one which44 implies the command of many books as well as of much leisure."

Seneca, the old Roman teacher, says: "Definite reading is profitable; miscellaneous reading is pleasant.... The reading of many authors and of all kinds of works has in it something vague and unstable."

Says Quintilian: "Every good writer is to be read, and diligently; and when the volume is finished, it is to be gone through again from the beginning."

Martin Luther, in his "Table Talk," says: "All who would study with advantage in any art whatsoever ought to betake themselves to the reading of some sure and certain books oftentimes over; for to read many books produceth confusion rather than learning, like as those who dwell everywhere are not anywhere at home."

"Reading," says Locke the philosopher, "furnishes the mind only with materials of knowledge; it is thinking that makes what are read over. We are of the ruminating kind, and it is not enough to cram ourselves with a great load of collections; unless we chew them over again, they will not give us strength and nourishment."

"Much reading," says Dr. Robert South,45 "is like much eating,—wholly useless without digestion."

"Desultory reading," writes Julius C. Hare, "is indeed very mischievous, by fostering habits of loose, discontinuous thought, by turning the memory into a common sewer for rubbish of all thoughts to flow through, and by relaxing the power of attention, which of all our faculties most needs care, and is most improved by it. But a well-regulated course of study will no more weaken the mind than hard exercise will weaken the body; nor will a strong understanding be weighed down by its knowledge, any more than oak is by its leaves or than Samson was by his locks. He whose sinews are drained by his hair must already be a weakling."[10]

Says Thomas Carlyle: "Learn to be good readers,—which is perhaps a more difficult thing than you imagine. Learn to be discriminative in your reading; to read faithfully, and with your best attention, all kinds of things which you have a real interest in,—a real, not an imaginary,—and which you find to be really fit for what you are engaged in. The most unhappy of all men is the man who cannot tell what he is going to do, who has 46got no work cut out for him in the world, and does not go into it. For work is the grand cure of all the maladies and miseries that ever beset mankind,—honest work, which you intend getting done."

Says Ralph Waldo Emerson: "The best rule of reading will be a method from nature, and not a mechanical one of hours and pages. It holds each student to a pursuit of his native aim, instead of a desultory miscellany. Let him read what is proper to him, and not waste his memory on a crowd of mediocrities. ... The three practical rules which I have to offer are: 1. Never read any book that is not a year old. 2. Never read any but famed books. 3. Never read any but what you like; or, in Shakspeare's phrase,—

'No profit goes where is no pleasure ta'en:

In brief, sir, study what you most affect.'"[11]

"Let us read good works often over," says another writer.[12] "Some skip from volume to volume, touching on all points, resting on none. We hold, on the contrary, that if a book be worth reading once, it is worth reading twice, and that if it stands a second reading, it may stand a third. This, indeed, 47is one great test of the excellence of books. Many books require to be read more than once, in order to be seen in their proper colors and latent glories, and dim-discovered truths will by-and-by disclose themselves.... Again, let us read thoughtfully; this is a great secret in the right use of books. Not lazily, to mumble, like the dogs in the siege of Corinth, as dead bones, the words of the author,—not slavishly to assent to his every word, and cry Amen to his every conclusion,—not to read him as an officer his general's orders, but to read him with suspicion, with inquiry, with a free exercise of your own faculties, with the admiration of intelligence, and not with the wonder of ignorance,—that is the proper and profitable way of reading the great authors of your native tongue."

Says Sir Arthur Helps: "There is another view of reading which, though it is obvious enough, is seldom taken, I imagine, or at least acted upon; and that is, that in the course of our reading we should lay up in our minds a store of goodly thoughts in well-wrought words, which should be a living treasure of knowledge always with us, and from which, at various times and amidst all the shifting of circumstances, we might be48 sure of drawing some comfort, guidance, and sympathy.... In any work that is worth carefully reading, there is generally something that is worth remembering accurately. A man whose mind is enriched with the best sayings of his own country is a more independent man, walks the streets in a town or the lanes in the country with far more delight than he otherwise would have, and is taught by wise observers of man and nature to examine for himself. Sancho Panza, with his proverbs, is a great deal better than he would have been without them; and I contend that a man has something in himself to meet troubles and difficulties, small or great, who has stored in his mind some of the best things which have been said about troubles and difficulties."[13]

And John Ruskin: "No book is worth anything which is not worth *much*; nor is it serviceable until it has been read, and reread, and loved, and loved again; and marked, so that you can refer to the passages you want in it, as a soldier can seize the weapons he needs in an armory, or a housewife bring the spice she needs from her store."

49

"I am not at all afraid," says Matthew Browne, "of urging overmuch the propriety of frequent, very frequent, reading of the same book. The book remains the same, but the reader changes; and the value of reading lies in the collision of minds. It may be taken for granted that *no* conceivable amount of reading could ever put me into the position with respect to his book—I mean as to intelligence only—in which the author strove to place me. I may read him a hundred times, and not catch the precise right point of view; and may read him a hundred and one times, and approach it the hundred and first. The driest and hardest book that ever was, contains an interest over and above what can be picked out of it, and laid, so to speak, on the table. It is interesting as my friend is interesting; it is a problem which invites me to closer knowledge, and *that* usually means better liking. He must be a poor friend that we only care to see once or twice, and then forget."[14]

"The great secret of reading consists in this," says Charles F. Richardson, "that it does not matter so much what we read, or 50how we read it, as what we think and how we think it. Reading is only the fuel; and, the mind once on fire, any and all material will feed the flame, provided only it have any combustible matter in it. And we cannot tell from what quarter the next material will come. The thought we need, the facts we are in search of, may make their appearance in the corner of the newspaper, or in some forgotten volume long ago consigned to dust and oblivion.... The mind that is not awake and alive will find a library a barren wilderness. Now, gather up the scraps and fragments of thought on whatever subject you may be studying,—for of course by a note-book I do not mean a mere receptacle for odds and ends, a literary dust-bin,—but acquire the habit of gathering everything whenever and wherever you find it, that belongs in your line or lines of study, and you will be surprised to see how such fragments will arrange themselves into an orderly whole by the very organizing power of your own thinking, acting in a definite direction. This is a true process of self-education; but you see it is no mechanical process of mere aggregation. It requires activity of thought; but without that, what is any reading but51mere passive amusement? And it requires method. I have myself a sort of literary book-keeping. I post my literary accounts, bringing together in proper groups the fruits of much casual reading."[15]

Edward Gibbon the historian tells us that a taste for books was the pleasure and glory of his life. "Let us read with method," he says, "and propose to ourselves an end to what our studies may point. The use of reading is to aid us in thinking."

Among practical suggestions to those who would read for profit, I have found nothing more pertinent than the following from the posthumous papers of Bryan Waller Procter: "Always read the preface to a book. It places you on vantage ground, and enables you to survey more completely the book itself. You frequently also discover the character of the author from the preface. You see his aims, perhaps his prejudices. You see the point of view from which he takes his pictures, the rocks and impediments which he himself beholds, and you steer accordingly.... Understand every word you read; if possible, every allusion of the author,—if practicable, while you are reading; 52if not, make search and inquiry as soon as may be afterward. Have a dictionary near you when you read; and when you read a book of travels, always read with a map of the country at hand. Without a map the information is vague and transitory.... After having read as much as your mind will easily retain, sum up what you have read,—endeavor to place in view the portion or subject that has formed your morning's study; and then reckon up (as you would reckon up a sum) the facts or items of knowledge that you have gained. It generally happens that the amount of three or four hours' reading may be reduced to and concentrated in half a dozen propositions. These are your gains,—these are the facts or opinions that you have acquired. You may investigate the truth of them hereafter. Although I think that one's general reading should extend over many subjects, yet for serious *study* we should confine ourselves to some branch of literature or science. Otherwise the mind becomes confused and enfeebled, and the thoughts, dissipated on many things, will settle profitably on none. A man whose duration of life is limited, and whose powers are limited also, should not aim at all things,53 but should content himself with a few. By such means he may master one, and become tolerably familiar perhaps with two or three arts or sciences. He may indeed even make valuable contributions to them. Without this economy of labor, he cannot produce any complete work, nor can he exhaust any subject."[16]

Every scholar is familiar with Lord Bacon's classification of books,—some "to be tasted, others to be swallowed, and some few to be chewed and digested: that is, some books are to be read only in parts; others to be read, but not curiously; and some few to be read wholly, and with diligence and attention." Coleridge's classification of the various kinds of readers is perhaps not quite so well known. He said that some readers are like jelly-bags,—they let pass away all that is pure and good, and retain only what is impure and refuse.

Another class he typified by a sponge; these are they whose minds suck all up, and give it back again, only a little dirtier. Others, again, he likened to an hour-glass, and their reading to the sand which runs in and out, and leaves no trace 54behind. And still others he compared to the slave in the Golconda mines, who retains the gold and the gem, and casts aside the dust and the dross. Charles C. Colton, the author of "Lacon," says there are three kinds of readers: first, those who read to think,—and they are rare; second, those who read to write,—and they are common; third, those who read to talk,—and they form the great majority. And Goethe, the greatest name in German literature, makes still a different classification: some readers, he tells us, enjoy without judgment; others judge without enjoyment; and some there are who judge while they enjoy, and enjoy while they judge.

In these days, when, so far as reading-matter is concerned, we are overburdened with an embarrassment of riches, we cannot afford to read, even in the books which we have chosen as ours, those things which have no relationship to our studies, which do not concern us, and which are sure to be forgotten as soon as read. The art of reading, says Philip Gilbert Hamerton in his admirable essay on "The Intellectual Life," "is to skip judiciously. The art is to skip all that does not concern us, whilst missing nothing that we really need. No external guidance can55 teach this; for nobody but ourselves can guess what the needs of our intellect may be. But let us select with decisive firmness, independently of other people's advice, independently of the authority of custom." And Charles F. Richardson, referring to the same subject, remarks: "The art of skipping is, in a word, the art of noting and shunning that which is bad, or frivolous, or misleading, or unsuitable for one's individual needs. If you are convinced that the book or the chapter is bad, you cannot drop it too quickly. If it is simply idle and foolish, put it away on that account,—unless you are properly seeking amusement from idleness and frivolity. If it is something deceitful and disingenuous, your task is not so easy; but your conscience will give you warning, and the sharp examination which should follow will tell you that you are in poor literary company."

56

CHAPTER III.

On the Value and Use of Libraries.

ALL round the room my silent servants wait,—
My friends in every season, bright and dim
Angels and seraphim
Come down and murmur to me, sweet and low,
And spirits of the skies all come and go
Early and late;
From the old world's divine and distant date,
From the sublimer few,
Down to the poet who but yester-eve
Sang sweet and made us grieve,
All come, assembling here in order due.
And here I dwell with Poesy, my mate,
With Erato and all her vernal sighs,
Great Clio with her victories elate,
Or pale Urania's deep and starry eyes.
BRYAN WALLER PROCTER.

LIBRARY is the scholar's workshop. To the teacher or professional man, a collection of good books is as necessary as a kit of tools to a carpenter. And yet I am aware that many persons are engaged in teaching,57 who have neither a library of their own, nor access to any other collection of books suitable to their use. There are others who, having every opportunity to secure the best of books,—with a public library near at hand offering them the free use of works most valuable to them,—yet make no effort to profit by these advantages. They care nothing for any books save the text-books indispensable to their profession, and for these only so far as necessity obliges them to do so. The libraries of many persons calling themselves teachers consist solely of school-books, many of which have been presented them by accommodating book-agents, "for examination with a view to introduction." And yet we hear such teachers talk learnedly about the introduction of English literature into the common schools of the country, and the necessity of cultivating among the children a wholesome love and taste for reading. If inquiry were made, we might discover that by a study of English literature these teachers understand some memoriter exercises in Shaw's "Manual" or Brooke's "Primer," and that, as to good reading, some there are who are entertained more deeply by Peck's "Bad Boy" than by Shakspeare's "Merchant of Venice." Talk not58 about directing and cultivating the reading-tastes of your pupils until you have successfully directed and cultivated your own! And the first step towards doing this is the selection and purchase of a library for yourself, which shall be all your own. A very few books will do, if they are of the right kind; and they must be *yours*. A borrowed book is but a cheap pleasure, an unappreciated and unsatisfactory tool. To know the true value of books, and to derive any satisfactory benefit from them, you must first feel the sweet delight of buying them,—you must know the preciousness of possession.

You plead poverty,—the insufficiency of your salary? But do you not spend for other things, entirely unnecessary, much more every year than the cost of a few books? The immediate outlay need not be large, the returns which you will realize will be great in proportion to your good judgment and earnestness. Not only will the possession of a good library add to your means of enjoyment and increase your capacity for doing good, it may, if you are worldly-minded,—and we all are,—put you in the way of occupying a more desirable position and earning a more satisfactory reward for your labors.

59

There are two kinds of books that you will need in your library: first, those which are purely professional, and are in the strictest sense the tools of your craft; second, those which belong to your chosen department of literature, and are to be regarded as your friends, companions, and counsellors. I cannot, of course, dictate to you what these books shall be. The lists given in the chapters which follow this are designed simply as suggestive aids. But in a library of fifty or even thirty well-chosen volumes you may possess infinite riches, and means for a lifetime of enjoyment; while, on the other hand, if your selection is injudicious, you may expend thousands of dollars for a collection of the odds and ends of literature, which will be only an incumbrance and a hindrance to you.

"I would urge upon every young man, as the beginning of his due and wise provision for his household," says John Ruskin, "to obtain as soon as he can, by the severest economy, a restricted, serviceable, and steadily—however slowly—increasing series of books for use through life; making his little library, of all the furniture in his room, the most studied and decorative piece; every volume having its assigned place, like a little60 statue in its niche, and one of the earliest and strictest lessons to the children of the house being how to turn the pages of their own literary possessions lightly and deliberately, with no chance of tearing or dog's-ears."[17]

And Henry Ward Beecher emphasizes the same thing, remarking that, among the early ambitions to be excited in clerks, workmen, journeymen, and indeed among all that are struggling up in life from nothing to something, the most important is that of forming and continually adding to a library of good books. "A little library, growing larger every year, is an honorable part of a man's history. It is a man's duty to have books. A library is not a luxury, but one of the necessaries of life."

"How much do you think we spend altogether on our libraries, public or private, as compared with what we spend on our horses?" asks another enthusiastic lover of books, already quoted. "If a man spends lavishly on his library, you call him mad,—a bibliomaniac. But you never call any one a horse-maniac, though men ruin themselves every day by their horses, and you do not hear of people ruining themselves by their books.... We talk of food for the mind, as of food for 61the body: now, a good book contains such food inexhaustibly; it is a provision for life, and for the best of us; yet how long most people would look at the best book before they would give the price of a large turbot for it! Though there have been men who have pinched their stomachs and bared their backs to buy a book, whose libraries were cheaper to them, I think, in the end than most men's dinners are. We are few of us put to such trial, and more the pity: for, indeed, a precious thing is all the more precious to us if it has been won by work or economy; and if public libraries were half as costly as public dinners, or books cost the tenth part of what bracelets do, even foolish men and women might sometimes suspect there was good in reading, as well as in munching and sparkling; whereas the very cheapness of literature is making even wise people forget that if a book is worth reading, it is worth buying."

"The truest owner of a library," says the author of "Hesperides," "is he who has bought each book for the love he bears to it,—who is happy and content to say, 'Here are my jewels, my choicest material possessions!'—who is proud to crown such assertion thus:62 'I am content that this library shall represent the use of the talents given me by Heaven!' That man's library, though not commensurate with his love for books, will demonstrate what he has been able to accomplish with his resources; it will denote economy of living, eagerness to possess the particles that compose his library, and quick watchfulness to seize them when means and opportunities serve. Such a man has built a temple, of which each brick has been the subject of curious and acute intelligent examination and appreciation before it has been placed in the sacred building."

"Every man should have a library!" exclaims William Axon. "The works of the grandest masters of literature may now be procured at prices that place them within the reach almost of the very poorest, and we may all put Parnassian singing-birds into our chambers to cheer us with the sweetness of their songs. And when we have got our little library we may look proudly at Shakspeare and Bacon and Bunyan, as they stand in our bookcase with other noble spirits, and one or two of whom the world knows nothing, but whose worth we have often tested. These may cheer and enlighten us, may inspire us63 with higher aims and aspirations, may make us, if we use them rightly, wiser and better men."[18]

Good old George Dyer, the friend of the poet Southey, as learned as he was benevolent, was wont to say: "Libraries are the wardrobes of literature, whence men, properly informed, may bring forth something for ornament, much for curiosity, and more for use." "Any library is an attraction," says the venerable A. Bronson Alcott; and Victor Hugo writes—

"A library implies an act of faith,
Which generations still in darkness hid
Sign in their night in witness of the dawn."

John Bright, the great English statesman and reformer, in a speech at the opening of the Birmingham Free Library a short time ago, remarked: "You may have in a house costly pictures and costly ornaments, and a great variety of decoration; yet, so far as my judgment goes, I would prefer to have one comfortable room well stocked with books to all you can give me in the way of decoration which the highest art can supply. The only subject of lamentation is—one feels that 64always, I think, in the presence of a library—that life is too short, and I am afraid I must say also that our industry is so far deficient that we seem to have no hope of a full enjoyment of the ample repast that is spread before us. In the houses of the humble a little library, in my opinion, is a most precious possession."

Jean Paul Richter, it is said, was always melancholy in a large library, because it reminded him of his ignorance.

"A library may be regarded as the solemn chamber in which a man can take counsel of all that have been wise and great and good and glorious amongst the men that have gone before him," said George Dawson, also at Birmingham. "If we come down for a moment and look at the bare and immediate utilities of a library, we find that here a man gets himself ready for his calling, arms himself for his profession, finds out the facts that are to determine his trade, prepares himself for his examination. The utilities of it are endless and priceless. It is, too, a place of pastime; for man has no amusement more innocent, more sweet, more gracious, more elevating, and more fortifying than he can 65find in a library. If he be fond of books, his fondness will discipline him as well as amuse him.... A library is the strengthener of all that is great in life, and the repeller of what is petty and mean; and half the gossip of society would perish if the books that are truly worth reading were read.... When we look through the houses of a large part of the middle classes of this country, we find there everything but what there ought most to be. There are no books in them worth talking of. If a question arises of geography, they have no atlases. If the question be when a great man was born, they cannot help you. They can give you a gorgeous bed, with four posts, marvellous adornments, luxurious hangings, and lacquered shams all round; they can give you dinners *ad nauseam*, and wine that one can, or cannot, honestly praise. But useful books are almost the last things that are to be found there; and when the mind is empty of those things that books can alone fill it with, then the seven devils of pettiness, frivolity, fashionableness, gentility, scandal, small slander, and the chronicling of small beer come in and take possession. Half this nonsense would be dropped if men would only understand the elevating influences of66their communing constantly with the lofty thoughts and high resolves of men of old times."

The author of "Dreamthorpe," filled with love and enthusiasm, discourses thus: "I go into my library, and all history unrolls before me. I breathe the morning air of the world while the scent of Eden's roses yet lingers in it, while it vibrates only to the world's first brood of nightingales and to the laugh of Eve. I see the pyramids building; I hear the shoutings of the armies of Alexander; I feel the ground shake beneath the march of Cambyses. I sit as in a theatre,—the stage is time; the play is the play of the world. What a spectacle it is! What kingly pomp, what processions file past, what cities burn to heaven, what crowds of captives are dragged at the chariot wheels of conquerors! I hiss, or cry 'Bravo,' when the great actors come on, shaking the stage. I am a Roman emperor when I look at a Roman coin. I lift Homer, and I shout with Achilles in the trenches. The silence of the unpeopled Assyrian plains, the out-comings and in-goings of the patriarchs,—Abraham and Ishmael, Isaac in the fields at eventide, Rebekah at the well, Jacob's guile, Esau's face reddened by desert 67sun-heat, Joseph's splendid funeral procession, —all these things I find within the boards of my Old Testament. What a silence in those old books as of a half-peopled world,—what bleating of flocks, what green pastoral rest, what indubitable human existence! Across brawling centuries of blood and war, I hear the bleating of Abraham's flocks, the tinkling of the bells of Rebekah's camels. O men and women, so far separated yet so near, so strange yet so well-known, by what miraculous power do I know you all? Books are the true Elysian fields, where the spirits of the dead converse; and into these fields a mortal may venture unappalled. What king's court can boast such company? What school of philosophy, such wisdom? The wit of the ancient world is glancing and flashing there. There is Pan's pipe, there are the songs of Apollo. Seated in my library at night, and looking on the silent faces of my books, I am occasionally visited by a strange sense of the supernatural. They are not collections of printed pages, they are ghosts. I take one down, and it speaks with me in a tongue not now heard on earth, and of men and things of which it alone possesses knowledge. I call myself a solitary, but sometimes I think 68I misapply the term. No man sees more company than I do. I travel with mightier cohorts around me than did ever Timour or Genghis Khan on their fiery marches. I am a sovereign in my library; but it is the dead, not the living, that attend my levees."

69

CHAPTER IV.

Books for every Scholar.

THESE books of mine, as you well know, are not drawn up here for display, however much the pride of the eye may be gratified in beholding them; they are on actual service.—SOUTHEY.

O assist teachers and scholars, and those who aspire to become such, in making judicious selection of world-famous books for their libraries, I submit the following list, which includes the greater part of all that is the very best and the most enduring in our language. It is not intended to embrace professional works, nor works suited merely for students of specialties. The books named are such as will grace the library of any scholar, no matter what his profession or his preferences; they are books which every teacher ought to know; they are 70books of which no one can ever feel ashamed. "The first thing naturally, when one enters a scholar's study or library," says Holmes, "is to look at his books. One gets a notion very speedily of his tastes and the range of his pursuits by a glance round his book-shelves." And, take my word for it, if you want a library of which you will be proud, you cannot be too careful as to the character of the books you put in it.

POETRY.

Chaucer's Poetical Works, or, if not the complete works, at least the "Canterbury Tales." In speaking of the great works in English Poetry, it is natural to mention Chaucer first, although, as a general rule, he should be one of the last read. "It is sufficient to say, according to the proverb, that *here is God's plenty*."—DRYDEN.

Spenser's Faerie Queene, not to be read through, but in selections. "We can scarcely comprehend how a perusal of the Faerie Queene can fail to insure to the true believer a succession of halcyon days."—HAZLITT.

The Works of William Shakspeare. The following editions of Shakspeare have been issued within the present century: The first Variorum (1813); The Variorum (1821); Singer's (10 vols. 1826); Knight's (8 vols. 1841); Collier's (8 vols. 1844); Verplanck's (3 vols. 1847); Hudson's (11 vols. 1857); Dyce's (6 vols. 1867); Mary Cowden Clarke's (2 vols. 1860); R. G. White's (12 vols. 711862); Clark and Wright's (9 vols. 1866); The Leopold Edition (1 vol. 1877); The Harvard Edition (20 vols. 1881); The Variorum (—vols. 1871—); Rolfe's School Shakspeare (1872-81); Hudson's School Shakspeare. "Above all poets, the mysterious dual of hard sense and empyrean fancy."—LORD LYTTON.

Ben Jonson's Dramatic and Poetical Works, to be read also in selections. "O rare Ben Jonson!"

Christopher Marlowe's Dramatic Works, especially "Tamburlaine," "Doctor Faustus," and "The Jew of Malta." "He had in him all those brave translunary things which the first poets did have."—DRAYTON.

Beaumont and Fletcher, and especially "The Faithful Shepherdess," a play "very characteristic of Fletcher, being a mixture of tenderness, purity, indecency, and absurdity."—HALLAM.

John Webster's Tragedies. "To move a horror skilfully, to touch a soul to the quick, to lay upon fear as much as it can bear, to wean and weary a life till it is ready to drop, and then step in with mortal instruments to take its last forfeit: this only a Webster can do."—CHARLES LAMB.

George Herbert's Poems. "In George Herbert there is poetry, and enough to spare; it is the household bread of his existence."—GÉORGE MACDONALD.

Milton's Poetical Works. The "Paradise Lost" was mentioned in the former list; but you cannot well do without his shorter poems also. "Milton almost requires a solemn service of music to be played before you enter upon him."—CHARLES LAMB.

Pope's Poetical Works. "Come we now to Pope, that prince of sayers of acute and exquisite things."—ROBERT CHAMBERS.

Dryden's Poems. "Dryden is even better than Pope. He has immense masculine energies."—IBID.

72*Goldsmith's Select Poems*. "No one like Goldsmith knew how to be at once natural and exquisite, innocent and wise, a man and still a child."—EDWARD DOWDEN.

The Poems of Robert Burns. "Burns should be my stand-by of a winter night."—J. H. MORSE.

Wordsworth's Select Poems. "Nearest of all modern writers to Shakspeare and Milton, yet in a kind perfectly unborrowed and his own."—COLERIDGE.

the Poems of Sir Walter Scott. "Walter Scott ranks in imaginative power hardly below any writer save Homer and Shakspeare."—GOLDWIN SMITH.

The Poems of Elizabeth Barrett Browning. "Mrs. Browning's 'Aurora Leigh' is, as far as I know, the greatest poem which the century has produced in any language."—RUSKIN.

Coleridge's Select Poems. "The Ancient Mariner," "Christabel," and "Genevieve." "These might be bound up in a volume of twenty pages, but they should be bound in pure gold."—STOPFORD BROOKE.

The Poems of John Keats. "No one else in English poetry, save Shakspeare, has in expression quite the fascinating felicity of Keats, his perfection of loveliness."—MATTHEW ARNOLD.

The Christian Year, by John Keble. "I am not a churchman,—I don't believe in planting oaks in flower-pots,—but such a poem as 'The Rosebud' makes one a proselyte to the culture it grows from."—DR. HOLMES.

Tennyson's Poems. "Tennyson is a born poet, that is, a builder of airy palaces and imaginary castles; he has chosen amongst all forms the most elegant, ornate, exquisite."—M. TAINE.

73*Longfellow's Poetical Works.* "In the pure, amiable, home-like qualities that reach the heart and captivate the ear, no one places Longfellow second."—THE CRITIC.

Bryant's Poetical Works. "The great characteristics of Bryant's poetry are its strong common-sense, its absolute sanity, and its inexhaustible imagination."—R. H. STODDARD.

The Poems of John G. Whittier. "The lyric poet of America, his poems are in the broadest sense national."—ANON.

In addition to the works named above, there are several collections of short poems and selections of poetry invaluable to the student. They are "infinite riches in little room." I name—

Bryant's Library of Poetry and Song.

Emerson's Parnassus.

Ward's English Poets.

Piatt's American Poetry and Art.

Appleton's Library of British Poetry.

Palgrave's Golden Treasury.

"A large part of what is best worth knowing in ancient literature, and in the literature of France, Italy, Germany, and Spain," says Lord Macaulay, "has been translated into our own tongue. I would not dissuade any person from studying either the ancient languages or the languages of modern Europe; but I would console those who have not time to make themselves linguists by assuring them74 that, by means of their own mother tongue, they may obtain ready access to vast intellectual treasures, to treasures such as might have been envied by the greatest linguists of the age of Charles the Fifth, to treasures surpassing those which were possessed by Aldus, by Erasmus, and by Melanchthon."

I name some of the treasures which you may thus acquire—

Homer's Iliad. Of this work, without which no scholar's library is complete, many translations have been made. The most notable are George Chapman's (1611), Pope's (1715), Tickell's (1715), Cowper's (1781), Lord Derby's (1867), Bryant's (1870). Americans will, of course, prefer Bryant's translation; but Derby's is more poetical, and the greatest scholars award the palm of merit to Chapman. Says Lowell: "Chapman has made for us the best poem that has yet been Englished out of Homer."

Æschylus. "Prometheus Bound" has been rendered into English verse by Elizabeth Barrett Browning, "Agamemnon" has been translated by Dean Milman, and the entire seven tragedies by Dean Potter. "The 'Prometheus' is a poem of the like dignity and scope as the Book of Job, or the Norse Edda."—EMERSON.

Aristophanes. The translation by John Hookham Frere is admirable. "We might apply to the pieces of Aristophanes the motto of a pleasant and acute adventurer in Goethe: 'Mad, but clever.'"—A. W. SCHLEGEL.

Virgil's Æneid. The best known translations of Virgil are Dryden's (1697), Christopher Pitt's75 (1740), John Conington's (1870), William Morris's (1876). Your choice among these will lie between the last two. "Virgil is far below Homer; yet Virgil has genius enough to be two men."—LORD LYTTON.

Horace's Odes, Epodes, and Satires. There are excellent translations by Conington, Lord Lytton, and T. Martin. "There is Horace, charming man of the world, who will condole with you feelingly on the loss of your fortune, ... but who will yet show you that a man may be happy with a vile modicum or *parva rura.*"—IBID.

Dante's Divina Commedia. Translated by Longfellow. "The finest narrative poem of modern times."—MACAULAY.

Goethe's Faust. Translated by Bayard Taylor. "What constitutes Goethe's glory is, that in the nineteenth century he did produce an epic poem—I mean a poem in which genuine gods act and speak."—H. A. TAINE.

Of the best poetry written in the modern foreign tongues, you will have no difficulty in finding excellent translations. There are good English editions of Dante, Petrarch, Ariosto, and Tasso; of Calderon and Camoens; of Molière, Corneille, Racine, and Victor

Hugo; and of Goethe and Schiller. And to make your collection complete for all the purposes of a scholar, you will want Longfellow's "Poets and Poetry of Europe," containing translations of the best short poems written in the modern European languages.

76

Of modern poetry, John Ruskin advises beginners to "keep to Scott, Wordsworth, Keats, Crabbe, Tennyson, the two Brownings, Lowell, Longfellow, and Coventry Patmore, whose 'Angel in the House' is a most finished piece of writing, and the sweetest analysis we possess of quiet modern domestic feeling.... Cast Coleridge at once aside as sickly and useless; and Shelley as shallow and verbose; Byron, until your taste is fully formed, and you are able to discern the magnificence in him from the wrong. Never read bad or common poetry, nor write any poetry yourself; there is, perhaps, rather too much than too little in the world already."

Says Frederic Harrison: "I am for the school of all the great men; and I am against the school of the smaller men. I care for Wordsworth as well as for Byron, for Burns as well as for Shelley, for Boccaccio as well as for Milton, for Bunyan as well as Rabelais, for Cervantes as much as for Dante, for Corneille as well as for Shakspeare, for Goldsmith as well as Goethe. I stand by the sentence of the world; and I hold that in a matter so human and so broad as the highest poetry, the judgment of the nations of Europe is pretty well settled.... The busy world may77 fairly reserve the lesser lights for the time when it knows the greatest well.... Nor shall we forget those wonderful idealizations of awakening thought and primitive societies, the pictures of other races and types of life removed from our own: all those primeval legends, ballads, songs, and tales, those proverbs, apologues, and maxims which have come down to us from distant ages of man's history,—the old idyls and myths of the Hebrew race; the tales of Greece, of the Middle Ages, of the East; the fables of the old and the new world; the songs of the Nibelungs; the romances of early feudalism; the 'Morte d'Arthur'; the 'Arabian Nights;' the ballads of the early nations of Europe."

PROSE.

In the following list I shall endeavor to name only the truly great and time-abiding books,—books to be used not simply as tools, but for the "building up of a lofty character," the turning of the soul inward upon itself, concentrating its forces, and fitting it for greater and stronger achievements. They embody the best thoughts of the best thinkers; and almost any one of them, if properly read78 and "energized upon," will furnish food for study, and meditation, and mind-growth, enough for the best of us.

ESSAYS, ETC.

The Works of Lord Bacon. (Popular edition.) "He seemed to me ever, by his work, one of the greatest men, and most worthy of admiration, that had been in many ages."—BEN JONSON.

Religio Medici, by Sir Thomas Browne. "One of the most beautiful prose poems in the language."—LORD LYTTON.

The Anatomy of Melancholy, by Robert Burton. Byron says that "if the reader has patience to go through the 'Anatomy of Melancholy,' he will be more improved for literary conversation than by the perusal of any twenty other works with which I am acquainted."

Montaigne's Essays. (Best edition.) "Montaigne comes in for a large share of the scholar's regard; opened anywhere, his page is sensible, marrowy, quotable."—A. BRONSON ALCOTT.

Areopagitica, by John Milton. "A sublime treatise, which every statesman should wear as a sign upon his hand and as frontlets between his eyes."—MACAULAY.

The Spectator. "The talk of Addison and Steele is the brightest and easiest talk that was ever put in print."—JOHN RICHARD GREEN.

Burke's Orations and Political Essays. "In amplitude of comprehension and richness of imagination, Burke was superior to every orator, ancient or modern."—LORD MACAULAY.

Webster's Best Speeches. "But after all is said, we come back to the simple statement that he was79 a very great man; intellectually, one of the greatest men of his age."—HENRY CABOT LODGE.

The Orations of Demosthenes. A good translation is that of Kennedy in Bohn's Classical Library.

Cicero's Orations; also Cicero's Offices, Old Age, Friendship, etc.

Plutarch's Lives. Arthur Hugh Clough's revision of Dryden's Plutarch. "Without Plutarch, no library were complete."—A. BRONSON ALCOTT.

The Six Chief Lives from Johnson's Lives of the Poets, edited by Matthew Arnold.

Boswell's Life of Samuel Johnson. "Scarcely since the days of Homer has the feat been equalled; indeed, in many senses, this also is a kind of heroic poem."—CARLYLE.

Charles Lamb's Essays. "People never weary of reading Charles Lamb."—ALEXANDER SMITH.

Carlyle's Works. "No man of his generation has done as much to stimulate thought."—ALFRED GUERNSEY.

Macaulay's Essays. "I confess to a fondness for books of this kind."—H. A. TAINE.

Froude's Short Studies on Great Subjects. "Models of style and clear-cut thought."—ANON.

The Works of Washington Irving. "In the department of pure literature the earliest classic writer of America."

The Autocrat of the Breakfast-Table, by Oliver Wendell Holmes. "Something more than an essayist; he is contemplative, discursive, poetical, thoughtful, philosophical, amusing, imaginative, tender—never didactic."—MACKENZIE.

Emerson's Essays. "A diction at once so rich and so homely as his, I know not where to match in these days of writing by the page; it is like home-spun cloth-of-gold."—J. R. LOWELL.

80

FICTION.

The novel, in its best form, I regard as one of the most powerful engines of civilization ever invented.

SIR JOHN HERSCHEL.

Novels are sweets. All people with healthy literary appetites love them,—almost all women; a vast number of clever, hard-headed men, judges, bishops, chancellors, mathematicians, are notorious novel-readers, as well as young boys and sweet girls, and their kind, tender mothers.

W. M. THACKERAY.

Robinson Crusoe, by Daniel Defoe. "'Robinson Crusoe' contains (not for boys, but for men) more religion, more philosophy, more psychology, more political economy, more anthropology, than are found in many elaborate treatises on these special subjects."—F. HARRISON.

Don Quixote de la Mancha, by Cervantes. "The work of Cervantes is the greatest in the world after Homer's Iliad, speaking of it, I mean, as a work of entertainment."—DR. JOHNSON.

Gulliver's Travels, by Dean Swift. "Not so indispensable, but yet the having him is much to be rejoiced in."—R. CHAMBERS.

The Vicar of Wakefield, by Goldsmith. "The blotting out of the 'Vicar of Wakefield,' from most minds, would be more grievous than to know that the island of Borneo had sunk in the sea."—IBID.

81

The Waverley Novels. If not all, at least the following: Ivanhoe; The Talisman; Kenilworth; The Monastery; The Abbot; Old Mortality; The Antiquary; Guy Mannering; The Bride of Lammermoor; The Heart of Midlothian.

Cooper's Leather-Stocking Tales.

Dickens's Novels. Not all, but the following: David Copperfield; Dombey and Son; Nicholas Nickleby; Old Curiosity Shop; Oliver Twist; and The Pickwick Papers.

Thackeray's Novels. Vanity Fair; Pendennis; The Newcomes; The Virginians; Henry Esmond.

George Eliot's Novels. Adam Bede; The Mill on the Floss; Romola; Middlemarch; Daniel Deronda.

Corinne, by Madame de Staël.

Telemachus, by Fénelon. (Hawkesworth's translation.)

Tom Jones, by Fielding. "We read his books as we drink a pure, wholesome, and rough wine, which cheers and fortifies us, and which wants nothing but bouquet."—H. A. TAINE.

Wilhelm Meister's Apprenticeship, by Goethe. (Carlyle's translation.)

Nathaniel Hawthorne's Novels. The Scarlet Letter; The Marble Faun; The Blithedale Romance; The House of Seven Gables.

Les Miserables, by Victor Hugo.

Hypatia and *Alton Locke*, by Charles Kingsley.

Uncle Tom's Cabin, by Mrs. Stowe. "We have seen an American woman write a novel of which a million copies were sold in all languages, and which had one merit, of speaking to the universal heart, and was read with equal interest to three audiences, namely, in the parlor, in the kitchen, and in the nursery of every house."—EMERSON.

Innocents Abroad, by Mark Twain.

82

Bulwer-Lytton's Novels. The Caxtons; My Novel; Zanoni; The Last of the Barons; Harold; The Last Days of Pompeii.

Jane Eyre, by Charlotte Brontë.

John Halifax, Gentleman, by Mrs. Craik.

This list might be readily extended; but I forbear, resolved rather to omit some meritorious works than to include any that are unworthy of the best companionship.

I close this chapter with Leigh Hunt's pleasant word-picture descriptive of his own library: "Sitting last winter among my books, and walled round with all the comfort and protection which they and my fireside could afford me,—to wit, a table of high-piled books at my back, my writing-desk on one side of me, some shelves on the other, and the feeling of the warm fire at my feet,—I began to consider how I loved the authors of those books; how I loved them too, not only for the imaginative pleasures they afforded me, but for their making me love the very books themselves, and delight to be in contact with them. I looked sideways at my Spenser, my Theocritus, and my Arabian Nights; then above them at my Italian Poets; then behind me at my Dryden and Pope, my Romances, and my Boccaccio; then on83 my left side at my Chaucer, who lay on my writing-desk; and thought how natural it was in Charles Lamb to give a kiss to an old folio, as I once saw him do to Chapman's Homer.... I entrench myself in my books, equally against sorrow and the weather. If the wind comes through a passage, I look about to see how I can fence it off by a better disposition of my movables; if a melancholy thought is importunate, I give another glance at my Spenser. When I speak of being in contact with my books, I mean it literally. I like to be able to lean my head against them.... The very perusal of the backs is a 'discipline of humanity.' There Mr. Southey takes his place again with an old Radical friend; there Jeremy Collier is at peace with Dryden; there the lion, Martin Luther, lies down with the Quaker lamb, Sewell; there Guzman d'Alfarache thinks himself fit company for Sir Charles Grandison, and has his claims admitted.... Nothing, while I live and think, can deprive me of my value for such treasures. I can help the appreciation of them while I last, and love them till I die; and perhaps I may chance, some quiet day, to lay my over-beating temples on a book, and so have the death I most envy."

84

CHAPTER V.

What Books Shall Young Folks Read?

HE greatest problem presented to the consideration of parents and teachers now-a-days is how properly to regulate and direct the reading of the children. There is no scarcity of reading-matter. The poorest child may have free access to books and papers, more than he can read. The publication of periodicals and cheap books especially designed to meet the tastes of young people has developed into an enterprise of vast proportions. Every day, millions of pages of reading matter designed for children are printed and scattered broadcast over the land. But unlimited opportunities often prove to be a damage and a detriment; and over-abundance, rather than scarcity, is to be deplored. As a general rule,85 the books read by young people are not such as lead to studious habits, or induce correct ideas of right living. They are intended simply to amuse; there are no elements of strength in them, leading up to a noble manhood. I doubt if in the future it can be said of any great statesman or scholar that his tastes had been formed, and his energies directed and sustained, through the influence of his early reading; but rather that he had attained success, and whatever of true nobility there is in him, in spite of such influence.

This was not always so. The experience of a few well-known scholars will illustrate. "From my infancy," says Benjamin Franklin, "I was passionately fond of reading, and all the money that came into my hands was laid out in the purchasing of books. I was very fond of voyages. My first acquisition was Bunyan's works in separate little volumes. I afterwards sold them to enable me to buy R. Burton's Historical Collections. They were small chapmen's books, and cheap; forty volumes in all. My father's little library consisted chiefly of books in polemic divinity, most of which I read. I have often regretted that at a time when I had such a thirst for86knowledge more proper books had not fallen in my way, since it was resolved I should not be bred to divinity. There was among them Plutarch's Lives, which I read abundantly, and I still think the time spent to great advantage. There was also a book of Defoe's called 'An Essay on Projects,' and another of Dr. Mather's, called 'An Essay to Do Good,' which perhaps gave me a turn of thinking that had an influence on some of the principal future events of my life. This bookish inclination at length determined my father to make me a printer.... I stood out some time, but at last was persuaded, and signed the indenture when I was yet but twelve years old.... I now had access to better books. An acquaintance with the apprentices of booksellers enabled me sometimes to borrow a small one, which I was careful to return soon, and clean. Often I sat up in my chamber the greatest part of the night, when the book was borrowed in the evening and to be returned in the morning, lest it should be found missing.... About this time I met with an odd volume of the 'Spectator.' I had never before seen any of them. I bought it, read it over and over, and was much delighted with it. I thought the writ87ing excellent, and wished if possible to imitate it. With that view I took some of the papers, and, making short hints of the sentiments in each sentence, laid them by a few days, and then, without looking at the book, tried to complete the papers again, by expressing each hinted sentiment at length, and as fully as it had been expressed before, in any suitable words that should occur to me. Then I compared my 'Spectator' with the original, discovered some of my faults, and corrected them....

"Now it was, that, being on some occasions made ashamed of my ignorance in figures, which I had twice failed learning when at school, I took Cocker's book on Arithmetic, and went through the whole by myself with the greatest ease. I also read Seller's and Sturny's book on Navigation, which made me acquainted with the little geometry it contains; but I never proceeded far in that science. I read about this time 'Locke on the Human Understanding,' and the 'Art of Thinking,' by Messrs. de Port Royal.

"While I was intent on improving my language, I met with an English Grammar (I think it was Greenwood's), having at the end of it two little sketches on the 'Arts of88 Rhetoric and Logic,' the latter finishing with a dispute in the Socratic method. And soon after, I procured Xenophon's 'Memorable Things of Socrates,' wherein there are many examples of the same method. I was charmed with it, adopted it, dropped my abrupt contradiction and positive argumentation, and put on the humble inquirer."[12]

Hugh Miller, that most admirable Scotchman and self-made man, relates a similar experience: "During my sixth year I spelled my way through the Shorter Catechism, the Proverbs, and the New Testament, and then entered upon the highest form in the dame's school as a member of the Bible class. But all the while the process of learning had been a dark one, which I slowly mastered, in humble confidence in the awful wisdom of the schoolmistress, not knowing whither it tended; when at once my mind awoke to the meaning of the most delightful of all narratives,—the story of Joseph. Was there ever such a discovery made before! I actually found out for myself that the art of reading is the art of finding stories in books; and from that moment reading became one of the most delightful of my amusements. I 89began by getting into a corner on the dismissal of the school, and there conning over to myself the new-found story of Joseph; nor did one perusal serve;—the other Scripture stories followed,—in especial, the story of Samson and the Philistines, of David and Goliath, of the prophets Elijah and Elisha; and after these came the New Testament stories and parables. Assisted by my uncles, too, I began to collect a library in a box of birch bark about nine inches square, which I found quite large enough to contain a great many immortal works: Jack the Giant-Killer, and Jack and the Bean-Stalk, and the Yellow Dwarf, and Blue Beard, and Sinbad the Sailor, and Beauty and the Beast, and Aladdin and the Wonderful Lamp, with several others of resembling character. Those intolerable nuisances, the useful-knowledge books, had not yet arisen, like tenebrious stars on the educational horizon, to darken the world, and shed their blighting influence on the opening intellect of the 'youthhood;' and so, from my rudimental books—books that made themselves truly such by their thorough assimilation with the rudimental mind—I passed on, without being conscious of break or line of division, to books on which the learned are90content to write commentaries and dissertations, but which I found to be quite as nice children's books as any of the others. Old Homer wrote admirably for little folk, especially in the Odyssey; a copy of which, in the only true translation extant,—for, judging from its surpassing interest, and the wrath of critics, such I hold that of Pope to be,—I found in the house of a neighbor. Next came the Iliad; not, however, in a complete copy, but represented by four of the six volumes of Bernard Lintot. With what power and at how early an age true genius impresses! I saw, even at this immature period, that no other writer could cast a javelin with half the force of Homer. The missiles went whizzing athwart his pages; and I could see the momentary gleam of the steel, ere it buried itself deep in brass and bull-hide. I next succeeded in discovering for myself a child's book, of not less interest than even the Iliad, which might, I was told, be read on Sabbaths, in a magnificent old edition of the 'Pilgrim's Progress,' printed on coarse whity-brown paper, and charged with numerous wood-cuts, each of which occupied an entire page, which, on principles of economy, bore letter-press on the other side....

91

"In process of time, I devoured, besides these genial works, Robinson Crusoe, Gulliver's Travels, Ambrose on Angels, the 'judgment chapter' in Howie's Scotch Worthies, Byron's Narrative, and the Adventures of Philip Quarll, with a good many other adventures and voyages, real and fictitious, part of a very miscellaneous collection of books made by my father. It was a melancholy library to which I had fallen heir. Most of the missing volumes had been with the master aboard his vessel when he perished. Of an early edition of Cook's Voyages, all the volumes were now absent, save the first; and a very tantalizing romance, in four volumes,—Mrs. Radcliffe's 'Mysteries of Udolpho,'—was represented by only the earlier two. Small as the collection was, it contained some rare books,—among the rest, a curious little volume entitled 'The Miracles of Nature and Art,' to which we find Dr. Johnson referring, in one of the dialogues chronicled by Boswell, as scarce even in his day, and which had been published, he said, some time in the seventeenth century by a bookseller whose shop hung perched on Old London Bridge, between sky and water. It contained, too, the only copy I ever saw of the 'Memoirs of a Protestant condemned to92 the Galleys of France for his Religion,'—a work interesting from the circumstance that, though it bore another name on its titlepage, it had been translated from the French for a few guineas by poor Goldsmith, in his days of obscure literary drudgery, and exhibited the peculiar excellences of his style. The collection boasted, besides, of a curious old book, illustrated by very uncouth plates, that detailed the perils and sufferings of an English sailor who had spent the best years of his life as a slave in Morocco. It had its volumes of sound theology, too, and of stiff controversy,—Flavel's Works, and Henry's Commentary, and Hutchinson on the Lesser Prophets, and a very old treatise on the Revelations, with the titlepage away, and blind Jameson's volume on the Hierarchy, with first editions of Naphtali, The Cloud of Witnesses, and the Hind Let Loose.... Of the works of fact and incident which it contained, those of the voyages were my special favorites. I perused with avidity the Voyages of Anson, Drake, Raleigh, Dampier, and Captain Woods Rogers; and my mind became so filled with conceptions of what was to be seen and done in foreign parts, that I wished myself big enough to be a sailor, that I might go and see coral93 islands and burning mountains, and hunt wild beasts, and fight battles."[20]

William and Robert Chambers, the founders of the great publishing-house of W. & R. Chambers, Edinburgh, were self-educated men. "At little above fourteen years of age," writes William, "I was thrown on my own resources. From necessity, not less than from choice, I resolved at all hazards to make the weekly four shillings serve for everything. I cannot remember entertaining the slightest despondency on the subject.... I made such attempts as were at all practicable, while an apprentice, to remedy the defects of my education at school. Nothing in that way could be done in the shop, for there reading was proscribed. But, allowed to take home a book for study, I gladly availed myself of the privilege. The mornings in summer, when light cost nothing, were my chief reliance. Fatigued with trudging about, I was not naturally inclined to rise; but on this and some other points I overruled the will, and forced myself to rise at five o'clock, and have a spell at reading until it was time to think of moving off,—my brother, when he was with me, doing the same. In this way I made 94some progress in French, with the pronunciation of which I was already familiar from the speech of the French prisoners of war at Peebles. I likewise dipped into several books of solid worth,—such as Smith's 'Wealth of Nations,' Locke's 'Human Understanding,' Paley's 'Moral Philosophy,' and Blair's 'Belles-Lettres,'—fixing the leading facts and theories in my memory by a note-book for the purpose. In another book I kept for years an accurate account of my expenses, not allowing a single halfpenny to escape record."

And Robert, the younger brother, confirms the story, with even more accurate attention to details. "My brother William and I," he says, "lived in lodgings together. Our room and bed cost three shillings a week.... I used to be in great distress for want of fire. I could not afford either that or a candle myself; so I have often sat by my landlady's kitchen fire,—if fire it could be called, which was only a little heap of embers,—reading Horace and conning my dictionary by a light which required me to hold the books almost close to the grate. What a miserable winter that was! Yet I cannot help feeling proud of my trials at that time. My brother and I—he then between fifteen and sixteen, I between95 thirteen and fourteen—had made a resolution together that we would exercise the last degree of self-denial. My brother actually saved money out of his income. I remember seeing him take five-and-twenty shillings out of a closed box which he kept to receive his savings; and that was the spare money of only a twelvemonth."[21]

Rev. Robert Collyer, whose name is known and honored by every American scholar, says: "Do you want to know how I manage to talk to you in this simple Saxon? I will tell you. I read Bunyan, Crusoe, and Goldsmith when I was a boy, morning, noon, and night. All the rest was task work; these were my delight, with the stories in the Bible, and with Shakspeare when at last the mighty master came within our doors.... I took to these as I took to milk, and, without the least idea what I was doing, got the taste for simple words into the very fibre of my nature. There was day-school for me until I was thirteen years old, and then I had to turn in and work thirteen hours a day.... I could not go home for the Christmas of 1839, and was feeling very sad about it all, for I was only a boy; 96and, sitting by the fire, an old farmer came in and said, 'I notice thou's fond o' reading, so I brought thee summat to read.' It was Irving's 'Sketch Book.' I had never heard of the work. I went at it, and was 'as them that dream.' No such delight had touched me since the old days of Crusoe. I saw the Hudson and the Catskills, took poor Rip at once into my heart, as everybody has, pitied Ichabod while I laughed at him, thought the old Dutch feast a most admirable thing; and long before I was through, all regret at my lost Christmas had gone down the wind, and I had found out there are books and books. That vast hunger to read never left me. If there was no candle, I poked my head down to the fire; read while I was eating, blowing the bellows, or walking from one place to another. I could read and walk four miles an hour. I remember while I was yet a lad reading Macaulay's great essay on Bacon, and I could grasp its wonderful beauty.... Now, give a boy a passion like this for anything, books or business, painting or farming, mechanism or music, and you give him thereby a lever to lift his world, and a patent of nobility, if the thing he does is noble."

97

It may be questioned whether, in these days of opportunities, it would be possible to find boys of thirteen and sixteen who would be able to read understandingly, much less appreciate and enjoy, those masterpieces of English literature so eagerly studied by Franklin and Hugh Miller and the Chambers brothers. Their mental appetites have been treated to a different kind of diet. If their minds have not been dwarfed and stunted by indulgence in what has been aptly termed "pen-poison," their tastes have been perverted and the growth of their reasoning powers checked by being fed upon the milk-and-water stuff recommended as harmless literature. They are inveterate devourers of stories, and novels, and the worthless material which is recommended as good reading, but which, in reality, is nothing but a "discipline of debasement." Better that children should not read at all, than read much of that which passes current now-a-days for entertaining reading.

All children like to read stories. The love of "the story," in some form or other, is indeed a characteristic of the human mind, and exists everywhere, in all conditions of life. But stories are the sweets of our mental98 existence, and only a few of the best and greatest have in them the elements which will lead to a strong and vigorous mind-growth. Constant feeding upon light literature—however good that literature may be in itself—will debilitate and corrupt the mental appetite of the child, much the same as an unrestrained indulgence in jam and preserves will undermine and destroy his physical health. In either case, if no result more serious occurs, the worst forms of dyspepsia will follow. Literary dyspepsia is the most common form of mental disease among us, and there is no knowing what may be the extent of its influence upon American civilization. Fifty per cent of the readers who patronize our great public libraries have weak literary stomachs; they cannot digest anything stronger than that insipid solution, the last society novel, or anything purer than the muddy decoctions poured out by the periodical press. When, of all the reading done in a public library, eighty per cent is of books in the different departments of fiction, I doubt whether, after all, that library is a public benefit. Yet this is but the natural result of the loose habits of reading which we encourage among our children, and cultivate in99 ourselves,—the habit of reading anything that comes to hand, provided only that it is entertaining.

How then shall we so order the child's reading as to avoid the formation of desultory and aimless habits?

Naturally, the earliest reading is the story,—simple, short, straightforward recitals of matters of daily occurrence, of the doings of children and their parents, their friends or their pets. "The Nursery," a little magazine published in Boston, contains an excellent variety of such stories. Now and then we may pick up a good book, too, for this class of readers; but there are many worthless books here, as elsewhere, and careful parents will look well into that which they buy. The illuminated covers are often the only recommendation of books of this kind. Numbers of them are made only for the holiday trade; the illustrations of many are from second-hand cuts; and the text is frequently written to fit the illustrations. A pure, fresh book for a little child is a treasure to be sought for and appreciated.

Very early in child-life comes the period of a belief in fairies; and the reading of fairy-stories is, to children, a very proper, nay,100 a very necessary thing. I pity the boy or girl who must grow up without having made intimate acquaintance with "Mother Goose," and the wonderful stories of "Jack the Giant-Killer," and "Blue Beard," and "Cinderella," and those other strange tales as old as the race itself, and yet new to every succeeding generation. They are a part of the inheritance of the English-speaking people, and belong, as a kind of birthright, to every intelligent child.

As your little reader advances in knowledge and reading-ability, he should be treated to stronger food. Grimm's "Household Stories" and the delightful "Wonder Stories" of Hans Christian Andersen, should form a part of the library of every child as he passes through the "fairy-story period" of his life; nor can we well omit to give him Charles Kingsley's "Water Babies," and "Alice's Adventures in Wonderland." And now, or later, as circumstances shall dictate, we may introduce him to that prince of all wonder-books, "The Arabian Nights' Entertainment," in an edition carefully adapted to children's reading. The tales related in this book "are not ours by birth, but they have nevertheless taken their place amongst the similar things of our101 own which constitute the national literary inheritance. Altogether, it is a glorious book, and one to which we cannot well show enough of respect."

And while your reader lingers in the great world of poetic fancy and child-wonder, let him revel for a while in those enchanting idyls and myths which delighted mankind when the race was young and this earth was indeed a wonder-world. These he may find, apparelled in a dress adapted to our modern notions of propriety, in Hawthorne's "Wonder Book" and "Tanglewood Tales," in Kingsley's "Greek Heroes," and, in a more prosaic form, in Cox's "Tales of Ancient Greece;" and in "The Story of Siegfried," and, later, in Morris's "Sigurd the Volsung," he may read the no less charming myths of our own northern ancestors, and the world-famous legend of the Nibelungen heroes. Then, by a natural transition, you advance into the border-land which lies between the world of pure fancy and the domains of sober-hued reality. You introduce your reader to some wholesome adaptations of those Mediæval Romances, which, with their one grain of fact to a thousand of fable, gave such noble delight to lords and ladies in the days of chivalry. These102 you will find in Sidney Lanier's "Boy's King Arthur" and "Boy's Mabinogion;" in "The Story of Roland," by the author of the present volume; and in Bulfinch's "Legends of Charlemagne" and "The Age of Chivalry."

Do you understand now to what point you have led your young reader? You have simply followed the order of nature and of human development, and you have gradually—almost imperceptibly even to yourself—brought him out of the world of child-wonder and fairy-land, through the middle ground of chivalric romance, to the very borders of the domains of history. He is ready and eager to enter into the realms of sober-hued truth; but I would not advise undue haste in this matter. The mediæval romances have inspired him with a desire to know more of those days when knights-errant rode over sea and land to do battle in the name of God and for the honor of their king, the Church, and the ladies; he wants to know something more nearly the truth than that which the minstrels and story-tellers of the Middle Ages can tell him. And yet he is not prepared for a sudden transition from romance to history. Let him read "Ivanhoe;" then give him Howard Pyle's "Story of Robin Hood" and Lanier's103 "Boy's Percy;" and if you care to allow him so much more fiction, let him read Madame Colomb's "Franchise" as translated and adapted by Davenport Adams in his "Page, Squire, and Knight." Can you withhold history longer from your reader? I think not. He will demand some authentic knowledge of Richard the Lion-hearted, and of King John, and of the Saxons and Normans, and of the Crusades, and of the Saracens, and of Charlemagne and his peers. Lose not your opportunity, but pass over with your pupil into the promised land. The transition is easy,—imperceptible, in fact,—and, leaving fiction and "the story" behind you, you enter the fields of truth and history. As for books, it is difficult now to advise; but there are Abbott's little histories,—give him the "History of Richard I." to begin with, then get the whole set for him. Yonge's "Young Folks' History of England," or Dickens's "Child's History" will also be in demand. The way is easy now, the road is open, you need no further guidance—only, keep straight ahead.

There are other books, of course, which the young reader will find in his way, and which it is altogether proper and necessary that he should read. For instance, there is "Robin104son Crusoe," without a knowledge of which the boy loses one of his dearest enjoyments. "How youth passed long ago, when there was no Crusoe to waft it away in fancy to the Pacific and fix it upon the lonely doings of the shipwrecked mariner, is inconceivable; but we can readily suppose that it must have been different," says Robert Chambers. And no substitute for the original Robinson will answer. Not one of the ten thousand tales of adventure recently published for boys will fill the niche which this book fills, or atone in the least for any neglect of its merits. "The Swiss Family Robinson" approaches nearest in excellence to Defoe's immortal creation, and may very profitably form a part of every boy's or girl's library. Then, among the really unexceptionable books, of the healthful, hopeful, truthful sort, I may name "Tom Brown's School Days at Rugby," Lamb's "Tales from Shakspeare," Mitchell's "About Old Story-Tellers;" the inimitable "Bodley Books," Bayard Taylor's "Boys of Other Countries," Abbott's "Franconia Stories," and a few others in the line of History or Travels, to be mentioned in future chapters. These I believe to be, in every sense, proper, wholesome books, free from all kinds of mannerisms,105 free from improper language, free from sickly sentiment and "gush;" and these, if not the most instructive books, are the sort of books which the child or youth should read as a kind of relish or supplement to the more methodical course of reading which I have elsewhere indicated.

In this careful direction of the child's reading, and in the cultivation of his literary taste, if you have succeeded in bringing him to the point which we have indicated, you have done much towards forming his character for life. There is little danger that bad books will ever possess any attractions for him; he will henceforth be apt to go right of his own accord, preferring the wholesome and the true to any of the flashy allurements of the "literary slums and grog-shops," which so abound and flourish in these days.

But perhaps the fundamental error in determining what books children shall read lies in the very popular notion that to read much, and to derive pleasure and profit from our reading, many books are necessary. And the greatest obstacle in the way of forming and directing a proper taste for good reading is to be found, not in the scarcity, but in the superabundance of reading matter. The great106 flood of periodical literature for young people is the worst hindrance to the formation of right habits in reading. Some of these periodicals are simply unadulterated "pen poison," designed not only to enrich their projectors, but to deprave the minds of those who read. Others are published, doubtless, from pure motives and with the best intentions; but, being managed by inexperienced or incapable editors, they are, at the best, but thin dilutions of milk-and-water literature, leading to mental imbecility and starvation. The periodicals fit to be placed in the hands of reading children may be numbered on half your fingers; and even these should not be read without due discrimination.

Too great a variety of books or papers placed at the disposal of inexperienced readers offers a premium to desultoriness, and fosters and encourages the habit of devouring every species of literary food that comes to hand. Hence we should beware not only of the bad, but of too great plenty of the good. "The benefit of a right good book," says Mr. Hudson, "all depends upon this, that its virtue just *soak* into the mind, and there become a living, generative force. To be running and rambling over a great many books, tasting a107 little here, a little there, and tying up with none, is good for nothing; nay, worse than nothing. Such a process of unceasing change is also a discipline of perpetual emptiness. The right method in the culture of the mind is to take a few choice books, and weave about them

'The fixed delights of house and home,
Friendship that will not break, and love that cannot roam.'

108

CHAPTER VI.

Hints on the Formation of School Libraries.

WHAT sort of reading are our schools planting an appetite for? Are they really doing anything to instruct and form the mental taste, so that the pupils on leaving them may be safely left to choose their reading for themselves? It is clear in evidence that they are far from educating the young to take pleasure in what is intellectually noble and sweet. The statistics of our public libraries show that some cause is working mightily to prepare them only for delight in what is both morally and intellectually mean and foul. It would not indeed be fair to charge our public schools with positively giving this preparation; but it is their business to forestall and prevent such a result. If, along with the faculty of reading, they cannot also impart some safeguards of taste and habit against such a result, will the system prove a success?—HENRY N. HUDSON.

UCH is being said, now-a-days, about the utility of school libraries; and in some instances much ill-directed, if not entirely misdirected, labor is being expended in their formation. Public libraries are not necessarily public benefits;109and school libraries, unless carefully selected and judiciously managed, will not prove to be unmixed blessings. There are several questions which teachers and school officers should seriously consider before setting themselves to the task of establishing a library; and no teacher who is not himself a knower of books, and a reader, should presume to regulate and direct the reading of others.

What are the objects of a school library? They are twofold: First, to aid in cultivating a taste for good reading; second, to supply materials for supplementary study and independent research. Now, neither of these objects can be attained unless your library is composed of books selected especially with reference to the capabilities and needs of your pupils. Dealing, as you do, with pupils of various degrees of intellectual strength, warped by every variety of moral influence and home training, the cultivation of a taste for good reading among them is no small matter. To do this, your library must contain none but truly good books. It is a great mistake to suppose that every collection of books placed in a schoolhouse is a library; and yet that is the name which is applied to many very inferior collections. It is no un110common thing to find these so-called libraries composed altogether of the odds and ends of literature,—of donations, entirely worthless to their donors; of second-hand school-books; of Patent Office Reports and other public documents; and of the dilapidated remains of some older and equally worthless collection of books: and with these you talk about cultivating a taste for good reading! One really good book, a single copy of "St. Nicholas," is worth more than all this trash. Get it out of sight at once! The value of a library—no matter for what purpose it has been founded—depends not upon the number of its books, but upon their character. And so the first rule to be observed in the formation of a school library is, Buy it at first hand, even though you should begin with a single volume, and shun all kinds of donations, unless they be donations of cash, or books of unquestionable value.

In selecting books for purchase, you will have an eye single to the wants of the students who are to use them. A school library should be in no sense a public circulating library. You cannot cater to the literary tastes of the public, and at the same time serve the best interests of your pupils. Books111relating to history, to biography, and to travel will form a very large portion of your library. These should be chosen with reference to the age and mental capacity of those who are to read them. No book should be bought merely because it is a good book, but because we know that it can be made useful in the attainment of certain desired ends. The courses of reading indicated in the following chapters of this work, it is hoped, will assist you largely in making a wise selection as well as in directing to a judicious use of books. For the selection of a book is only half of your duty: the profitable use of it is the other half; and this lesson should be early taught to your pupils.

If, through means of your school library or otherwise, you succeed in enlisting the interest of a young person in profitable methodical reading, you have accomplished a great deal towards the forwarding of his education and the formation of his character. It is a great mistake to suppose that a boy of twelve cannot pursue a course of reading in English history; if properly directed and encouraged, he will enjoy it far better than the perusal of the milk-and-water story-books which, under the guise of "harmless juvenile litera112ture," have been placed in his hands by well-meaning teachers or parents.

In a former chapter I have shown you how, with a library of only fifty volumes, you may have in your possession the very best of all that the world's master-minds have ever written,—food, as I have said, for study, and meditation, and mind growth enough for a lifetime. Such a library is worth more than ten thousand volumes of the ordinary "popular" kind of books. So, also, the reading of a very few books, carefully and methodically, by your pupils—the constant presence of the very best books in our language, and the exclusion of the trashy and the vile—will give them more real enjoyment and infinitely greater profit than the desultory or hasty reading of many volumes. A small library is to be despised only when it contains inferior books.

113

CHAPTER VII.

Courses of Reading in History.

HISTORY, at least in its state of ideal perfection, is a compound of poetry and philosophy.—MACAULAY.

Let us search more and more into the Past; let all men explore it as the true fountain of knowledge, by whose light alone, consciously or unconsciously employed, can the Present and the Future be interpreted or guessed at.—CARLYLE.

History is a voice forever sounding across the centuries the laws of right and wrong. Opinions alter, manners change, creeds rise and fall; but the moral law is written on the tablets of eternity.... Justice and truth alone endure and live. Injustice and falsehood may be long-lived, but doomsday comes at last to them in French revolutions and other terrible ways. That is one lesson of history. Another is, that we should draw no horoscopes; that we should expect little, for what we expect will not come to pass.—FROUDE.

The student is to read history actively and not passively; to esteem his own life the text, and books the commentary. Thus compelled, the Muse of history will utter oracles, as never to those who do not respect themselves. I have no114 expectation that any man will read history aright who thinks that what was done in a remote age, by men whose names have resounded far, has any deeper sense than what he is doing to-day.... The instinct of the mind, the purpose of nature, betrays itself in the use we make of the signal narrations of history.—EMERSON.

venture to propose the following courses of reading in history. Properly modified with reference to individual needs and capabilities, these lists will prove to be safe helps and guides to younger as well as older readers, to classes in high schools and colleges as well as private students and specialists. To read all the works here mentioned, as carefully and critically as the nature of their contents demands, would require no inconsiderable portion of one's reading lifetime. Such a thing is not expected. The wise teacher or the judicious scholar will select from the list that which is most proper for him, and which best meets his wants, or aids him most in the pursuit of his native aim.

The titles, so far as possible, are given in chronological order. Those printed in *italics* are of books indispensable for purposes of reference; those printed in SMALL CAPITALS are of works especially adapted to younger readers.

115

I. GREEK HISTORY.

Dictionaries.

No reader can well do without a good classical dictionary. The following are recommended as the best—

Anthon: *Classical Dictionary.*

Smith: *Student's Classical Dictionary.*

—— *Dictionary of Greek and Roman Antiquities.*

Ginn & Heath's *Classical Atlas.*

Kiepert's *Schulatlas.*

General Histories.

Cox: General History of Greece.

Smith: Smaller History of Greece.

Felton: Ancient and Modern Greece.

Yonge: YOUNG FOLKS' HISTORY OF GREECE.

Grote: *History of Greece* (12 vols.).

Curtius: *History of Greece* (5 vols.); translated from the German, by A. W. Ward.

J. A. St. John: Ancient Greece.

Mythology.

Dwight: *Grecian and Roman Mythology.*

Murray: Manual of Mythology.

Keightley: *Classical Mythology.*

Gladstone: Juventus Mundi.

Ruskin: The Queen of the Air.

Cox: TALES OF ANCIENT GREECE.

Kingsley: THE GREEK HEROES.

Hawthorne: THE WONDER BOOK.

—— TANGLEWOOD TALES.

116

Miscellaneous.

Homer's Iliad and Odyssey. Chapman's translation is the best. Of the later versions, that of Lord Derby is preferable.

Church: STORIES FROM HOMER.

Butcher and Lang's prose translation of the Odyssey.

Collins: The Iliad and the Odyssey (two volumes of "Ancient Classics for English Readers").

Gladstone: Homer.

De Quincey: Homer and the Homeridæ (essay in "Literary Criticism").

Fénelon: TELEMACHUS (translated by Hawkesworth).

Benjamin: Troy.

Goethe: Iphigenia in Tauris (drama, Swanwick's translation).

The student of this period is referred also to Dr. Schliemann's works: Ilios, Troja, and Mykenai.

Church: STORIES FROM HERODOTUS.

Swayne: Herodotus (Ancient Classics).

Brugsch Bey: History of Egypt.

Freeman: Historical Essays (2d series).

Ebers: Uarda (romance, descriptive of Egyptian life and manners fourteen centuries before Christ).

—— The Daughter of an Egyptian King (five centuries before Christ).

Smith: *Student's History of the East.*

Cox: The Greeks and the Persians.

Abbott: THE HISTORY OF DARIUS THE GREAT.

—— THE HISTORY OF XERXES THE GREAT.

Sankey: The Spartan Supremacy.

117

Bulwer: Pausanias the Spartan (romance, 475 B.C.).

Glover: Leonidas (epic poem).
Croly: The Death of Leonidas (poem).
Robert Browning: Pheidippides (poem in "Dramatic Idyls").
Lloyd: The Age of Pericles (fifth century before Christ).
Cox: The Athenian Empire.
Landor: Pericles and Aspasia (in "Imaginary Conversations").
Mrs. L. M. Child: Philothea (romance of the time of Pericles).
Curteis: The Macedonian Empire.
Abbott: THE HISTORY OF ALEXANDER THE GREAT.
Butcher: Demosthenes (Classical Writers).
Greenough: Apelles and his Contemporaries (a romance of the time of Alexander).
Dryden: Alexander's Feast (poem).
Bickersteth: Caubul (poem).

Literature.

Mahaffy: *History of Greek Literature.*
Schlegel: History of Dramatic Literature (first fourteen chapters).
Church: STORIES FROM THE GREEK TRAGEDIANS.
Copleston: Æschylus (Ancient Classics).
Mrs. Browning: Prometheus Bound (an English version of the great tragedy).
Bishop Milman: Agamemnon.
Collins: Sophocles (Ancient Classics).
De Quincey: The Antigone of Sophocles (essay in "Literary Criticism").
Donne: Euripides (Ancient Classics).
Froude: Sea Studies (essay in "Short Studies on Great Subjects").118 Collins: Aristophanes (Ancient Classics).
Mitchell: The Clouds of Aristophanes.
De Quincey: Theory of Greek Tragedy (essay in "Literary Criticism").
Brodribb: Demosthenes (Ancient Classics).
Collins: Plato (Ancient Classics).
Jowett: The Dialogues of Plato (4 vols.).
The Phædo of Plato (Wisdom Series).
Plato: The Apology of Socrates.
A Day in Athens with Socrates.
Plutarch: On the Dæmon of Socrates (essay in the "Morals").
Grant: Xenophon (Ancient Classics).
Collins: Thucydides (Ancient Classics).

Life and Manners.

For a study of social life and manners in Greece, read or refer to the following—
Becker: Charicles (romance, with copious notes and excursuses).
Mahaffy: Social Life in Greece.
—— Old Greek Life.
Guhl and Koner: Life of the Greeks and Romans.

Special Reference.

Draper: History of the Intellectual Development of Europe (vol. i.).
Clough: *Plutarch's Lives.*
Kaufman: THE YOUNG FOLKS' PLUTARCH.
White: PLUTARCH FOR BOYS AND GIRLS.

It is good exercise, good medicine, the reading of Plutarch's books,—good for to-day as it was in times preceding ours, salutary for all times.—A. BRONSON ALCOTT.

119

II. ROMAN HISTORY.

For purposes of reference the following books, already mentioned in the course of Greek History, are indispensable—

Anthon: *Classical Dictionary.*

Smith: *Dictionary of Greek and Roman Antiquities.*

Ginn & Heath: *Classical Atlas.*

Murray: *Manual of Mythology.*

General Histories.

Smith: Smaller History of Rome.

Merivale: Students' History of Rome.

Yonge: YOUNG FOLKS' HISTORY OF ROME.

Creighton: History of Rome.

For the period preceding the Empire—

Mommsen: *History of Rome* (4 vols.).

Abbott: THE HISTORY OF ROMULUS.

Church: STORIES FROM VIRGIL.

—— STORIES FROM LIVY.

Macaulay: Horatius (poem in "Lays of Ancient Rome").

Arnold: History of Rome.

Ihne: Early Rome.

Shakspeare: The Tragedy of Coriolanus (490 B.C.).

Macaulay: Virginia (poem in "Lays of Ancient Rome," 459 B.C.).

Abbott: THE HISTORY OF HANNIBAL.

Smith: Rome and Carthage.

Dale: Regulus before the Senate (poem, 256 B.C.).

Beesly: The Gracchi, Marius, and Sulla.

Mrs. Mitchell: Spartacus to the Gladiators (poem, 73 B.C.).

120

For the period of the Cæsars and the early Empire—

Merivale: *History of the Romans* (4 vols.).

—— The Roman Triumvirates.

Abbott: THE HISTORY OF JULIUS CÆSAR.

Addison: The Tragedy of Cato (drama).

Froude: Cæsar; a Sketch.

Trollope: Life of Cicero.

Ben Jonson: Catiline (drama).

Beaumont and Fletcher: The False One (drama).

Abbott: THE HISTORY OF CLEOPATRA.

Shakspeare: The Tragedy of Julius Cæsar.

—— Antony and Cleopatra.

Capes: The Early Empire.

De Quincey: The Cæsars.

Ben Jonson: The Poetaster (drama, time of Augustus).

Wallace: Ben Hur (romance, time of Tiberius).

Longfellow: The Divine Tragedy (poem).

Ben Jonson: Sejanus, his Fall (drama, time of Tiberius).

Becker: Gallus (romance, with notes, time of Tiberius).

Schele De Vere: The Great Empress (romance, time of Nero).

Abbott: THE HISTORY OF NERO.

W. W. Story: Nero (drama).

Hoffman: The Greek Maid at the Court of Nero (romance).

Farrar: Seekers after God (Seneca, Epictetus).

Wiseman: The Church of the Catacombs (romance, time of the Persecutions).

Mrs. Charles: The Victory of the Vanquished (romance).

121

Church and Brodribb: Pliny's Letters (Ancient Classics).

Bulwer: The Last Days of Pompeii (romance, time of Vespasian).
Massinger: The Roman Actor (drama, time of Domitian).
—— The Virgin Martyr (drama).
Dickinson: The Seed of the Church.
De Mille: Helena's Household.
Lockhart: Valerius.
The last three works are romances, depicting life and manners in the time of Trajan.
For the period of the later Empire and the decline of the Roman power—
Curteis: History of the Roman Empire (395-800).
Gibbon: *Decline and Fall of the Roman Empire.*
Ebers: The Emperor (romance, time of Hadrian).
Capes: The Age of the Antonines.
Watson: Marcus Aurelius Antoninus.
Hodgkin: Italy and her Invaders.
William Ware: Zenobia (romance, A.D. 266).
—— Aurelian (romance, A.D. 275).
Ebers: Homo Sum (romance, A.D. 330).
Kouns: Arius the Libyan (romance, A.D. 336).
Aubrey De Vere: Julian the Apostate (drama, A.D. 363).
Beaumont and Fletcher: Valentinian (drama, A.D. 375).
Edward Everett: Alaric the Visigoth; and Mrs. Hemans: Alaric in Italy (poems, A.D.410).
Kingsley: Hypatia (romance, A.D. 415).
Mrs. Charles: Conquering and to Conquer (romance, A.D. 418).
122
Mrs. Charles: Maid and Cleon (romance of Alexandria, A.D. 425).
Kingsley: Roman and Teuton.
Church: The Beginning of the Middle Ages.

Literature.

Simcox: History of Roman Literature.
Schlegel: History of Dramatic Literature.
Collins: Livy (Ancient Classics).
Mallock: Lucretius (Ancient Classics).
Trollope: Cæsar (Ancient Classics).
Collins: Cicero (Ancient Classics).
Morris: The Æneid of Virgil.
Collins: Virgil, Ovid, Lucian (three volumes of Ancient Classics).
Epictetus: Selections from Epictetus.
Jackson: Apostolic Fathers (Early Christian Literature Primers).

Special Reference.

Clough: *Plutarch's Lives.*
White: PLUTARCH FOR BOYS AND GIRLS.
Kaufman: THE YOUNG FOLKS' PLUTARCH.
Coulange: *The Ancient City.*
Draper: *History of the Intellectual Development of Europe.*
Lecky: *History of European Morals.*
Milman: History of Christianity.
Stanley: History of the Eastern Church.
Fisher: Beginnings of Christianity.
Döllinger: The First Age of Christianity.
Montalembert: The Monks of the West.
Reber: History of Ancient Art.
Hadley: Lectures on Roman Law.
Maine: Ancient Law.
123

III. MEDIÆVAL AND MODERN HISTORY.

This course has been prepared with special reference to English history. The right-hand column, headed Collateral Reading, will assist students desiring to extend their reading so as to embrace the history of Continental Europe. The figures affixed to some of the titles indicate, as nearly as is thought necessary, the time covered or treated of by the work mentioned. Historical romances and other prose works of fiction are designated thus (*); dramas thus (†; other poems thus (‡).

ENGLISH HISTORY. | COLLATERAL READING.

General Histories.

KNIGHT: *History of England* (9 vols.).
YONGE: YOUNG FOLKS' HISTORY OF ENGLAND.
DICKENS: CHILD'S HISTORY OF ENGLAND.
STRICKLAND: *Lives of the Queens of England* (7 vols.).
PEARSON: *Historical Atlas of England.*

WHITE: History of France.
LEWIS: Students' History of Germany.
HUNT: History of Italy.
YONGE: YOUNG FOLKS' HISTORY OF FRANCE.
KIRKLAND: SHORT HISTORY OF FRANCE.
HALLAM: View of the State of the Middle Ages.

The Anglo-Saxon Period.

GREEN: History of the English People, book i.
MRS. ARMITAGE: The Childhood of the English Nation.
GREEN: The Making of England.
124PALGRAVE: History of the Anglo-Saxons.
—— ‡Paulinus and Edwin.
TURNER: *History of the Anglo-Saxons.*
GRANT ALLEN: Anglo-Saxon Britain.
ABBOTT: ALFRED THE GREAT.
HUGHES: Life of Alfred the Great.
THIERRY: The Conquest of England by the Normans.
ABBOTT: WILLIAM THE CONQUEROR.
GREEN: The Conquest of England.
FREEMAN: *History of the Norman Conquest of England.*

GUIZOT: History of France, Vol. i.
JAMES: History of Charlemagne.
BRYCE: The Holy Roman Empire.
CUTTS: Scenes and Characters of the Middle Ages.
JOHNSON: The Normans in Europe.
CARLYLE: The Early Kings of Norway.
ANDERSON: Norse Mythology.
LETTSOM: ‡The Nibelungenlied.
DASENT: The Burnt Njal.
BALDWIN: *THE STORY OF SIEGFRIED.
MALLET: Northern Antiquities.

MRS. CHARLES: *Early Dawn (romance of the Roman occupation of Britain).
COWPER: ‡Boadicea.
LANIER: *THE BOY'S KING ARTHUR.
LOWELL: ‡The Vision of Sir Launfal.
TENNYSON: ‡The Idylls of the King.
SCOTT: ‡Sir Tristram.
TAYLOR: †Edwin the Fair.

JAMES: History of Chivalry.
BULFINCH: *The Age of Chivalry.
LANIER: *KNIGHTLY LEGENDS OF WALES.
LUDLOW: Popular Epics of the Middle Ages.
BULFINCH: Legends of Charlemagne.

BULWER: *Harold, the Last of the Saxons (1066).

TENNYSON: †Harold; a Drama.

LEIGHTON: †The Sons of Godwin.

KINGSLEY: *Hereward, the Last of the Saxons.

BALDWIN: *THE STORY OF ROLAND.

ARIOSTO: ‡Orlando Furioso.

LOCKHART: ‡Spanish Ballads.

YONGE: Christians and Moors in Spain.

SOUTHEY: Chronicles of the Cid.

TENNYSON: ‡Godiva (1040).

The Age of Feudalism.

JOHNSON: The Norman Kings and the Feudal System.

GREEN: History of the English People, books ii. and iii.

125PALGRAVE: ‡Death in the Forest (1100).

ABBOTT: RICHARD I.

HUME: History of England.

FROUDE: Life and Times of Thomas Becket.

AUBREY DE VERE: †St. Thomas of Canterbury.

JAMES: Life of Richard Cœur de Lion.

FROUDE: A Bishop of the Twelfth Century (1190).

STUBBS: The Early Plantagenets.

PYLE: THE STORY OF ROBIN HOOD.

SCOTT: *The Talisman (1193).

—— *Ivanhoe (1194).

JAMES: Forest Days (1214).

SHAKSPEARE: †King John (1215).

DRAYTON: †The Barons' Wars.

GUIZOT: History of France, vol. ii.

COX: The Crusades.

MICHAUD: History of the Crusades.

GRAY: The Children's Crusade.

GAIRDNER: Early Chroniclers of Europe.

OLIPHANT: Francis of Assisi.

ADAMS: *PAGE, SQUIRE, AND KNIGHT(1180).

HENTY: *THE BOY KNIGHT (1188).

SCOTT: *The Betrothed.

YONGE: *Richard the Fearless.

JAMES: *Philip Augustus.

SCOTT: *Count Robert of Paris.

HALE: *In his Name.

PAULI: Life of Simon de Montfort (1215).

PEARSON: English History in the Fourteenth Century.

YONGE: *The Prince and the Page (1280).

GRAY: ‡The Bard (1282).

CUNNINGHAM: *Sir Michael Scott (1300).

PORTER: *The Scottish Chiefs.

AGUILAR: *The Days of†‡ Bruce.

CAMPBELL: ‡The Battle of Bannockburn.

SCOTT: ‡The Lord of the Isles (1307).

MARLOWE: †Edward II. (1327).

WARBURTON: Edward III. (1327-77).

ABBOTT: RICHARD II.

LANIER: THE BOY'S FROISSART.

SOUTHEY: †Wat Tyler (1381)

CAMPBELL: ‡Wat Tyler's Address to

KINGSLEY: †The Saint's Tragedy (1220).

BROWNING: ‡Sordello (1230).

KINGTON-OLIPHANT: Frederick II. (1250).

GUIZOT: History of France, vol. iii.

HEMANS: †The Vespers of Palermo (1282).

BOKER: †Francesca di Rimini (1300).

SCHILLER: †Wilhelm Tell.

BULWER: Rienzi, the Last of the Tribunes (1347).

BYRON: †Marino Faliero (1355).

JAMISON: Life of Bertrand du Guesclin.

LORD HOUGHTON: ‡Bertrand du Guesclin (1380).

the King.

SHAKSPEARE: †Richard II. (1399)

BESANT AND RICE: Life of Whittington.

PERCY: ‡The Ballad of Chevy Chase.

GAIRDNER: The Houses of Lancaster and York.

EDGAR: The Wars of the Roses.

GREEN: History of the English People, book iv.

SHAKSPEARE: †King Henry IV.

Yonge: *The Caged Lion (1406).

TOWLE: History of Henry V.

EWALD: The Youth of Henry V. (in "Stories from the State Papers").

GAIRDNER: The Lollards.

DRAYTON: ‡The Battle of Agincourt (1415).

SHAKSPEARE: †King Henry VI.

BULWER: *The Last of the Barons (1460).

GAIRDNER: History of Richard III.

—— The Paston Letters.

SHAKSPEARE: †King Richard III.

ABBOTT: HISTORY OF RICHARD III.

HUTTON: James and Philip Van Artevelde.

126TAYLOR: †Philip Van Artevelde (1382).

MRS. BRAY: Joan of Arc and the Times of Charles VII. of France.

SOUTHEY: ‡Joan of Arc.

CALVERT: ‡The Maid of Orleans.

BROWNING: †Luria (1405).

JAMES: *Agincourt.

Kirk: History of Charles the Bold.

SCOTT: *Quentin Durward (1450).

BYRON: †The two Foscari (1457).

HERZ: ‡King René's Daughter.

SCOTT: *Anne of Geierstein.

VICTOR HUGO: *The Hunchback of Notre Dame.

BROWNING: †The Return of the Druses.

MACAULAY: Essay on Machiavelli.

Modern England.

BIRCHALL: England under the Tudors.

GREEN: History of the English People, books v. and vi.

127MANNING: The Household of Sir Thomas More.

SCOTT: †Marmion (1513).

JAMES: *Darnley (1520).

FROUDE: History of England from the Fall of Wolsey to the Death of Elizabeth.

MÜHLBACH: *Henry VIII. and Catherine Parr.

SHAKSPEARE: †King Henry VIII.

GEIKIE: History of the English Reformation.

MILMAN: †Anne Boleyn (1536).

AINSWORTH: *Tower Hill (1538).

EWALD: Stories from the State Papers.

MARK TWAIN: *THE PRINCE AND THE PAUPER (1548).

AUBREY DE VERE: †Mary Tudor.

TENNYSON: †Queen Mary.

SCOTT: ‡Lay of the Last Minstrel.

MANNING: *Colloquies of Edward

PRESCOTT: The History of Ferdinand and Isabella.

ANITA GEORGE: Isabel the Catholic.

IRVING: The Conquest of Granada.

—— The Alhambra.

AGUILAR: *The Edict (1492).

ROBERTSON: History of Charles V.

SEEBOHM: Era of the Protestant Revolution.

FISHER: History of the Reformation.

YONGE: *The Dove in the Eagle's Nest (1519).

MRS. CHARLES: *Chronicles of the Schönberg-Cotta Family.

GEORGE ELIOT: *Romola.

READE: *The Cloister and the Hearth.

MRS. STOWE: *Agnes of Sorrento.

Osborne (1554).

ROWE: †Lady Jane Grey (1554).

AINSWORTH: *The Tower of London (1554).

ABBOTT: HISTORY OF QUEEN ELIZABETH.

CREIGHTON: The Age of Elizabeth.

SCOTT: *Kenilworth (1560).

MACAULAY: Essays on Lord Burleigh and Bacon.

TOWLE: DRAKE, THE SEA KING OF DEVON.

ABBOTT: HISTORY OF MARY QUEEN OF SCOTS.

SCOTT: *The Monastery and The Abbot.

128YONGE: *Unknown to History (1587).

SWINBURNE: †Chastelard.

—— †Bothwell.

—— †Mary Stuart (1587).

SCHILLER: †Marie Stuart (1587).

MELINE: Life of Mary Queen of Scots (Catholic).

KINGSLEY: *Westward Ho!

WORDSWORTH: ‡The White Doe of Rylstone.

MACAULAY: ‡The Armada.

TENNYSON: ‡The Revenge.

TOWLE: SIR WALTER RALEGH.

LANDOR: Elizabeth and Burleigh (in "Imaginary Conversations").

GREEN: History of the English People, book vii.

CORDERY AND PHILLPOTT: King and Commonwealth.

GARDINER: The Puritan Revolution.

AINSWORTH: *Guy Fawkes (1605).

SCOTT: *The Fortunes of Nigel.

AINSWORTH: *The Spanish Match (1620).

ABBOTT: HISTORY OF CHARLES I.

LETITIA E. LANDON: ‡The Covenanters (1638).

MARRYAT: *THE CHILDREN OF THE NEW FOREST.

SCOTT: ‡Rokeby (1644).

—— *Legend of Montrose (1646).

PRAED: *Marston Moor (1644).

CARLYLE: History of Oliver Cromwell.

GUIZOT: History of the English Revolution.

129

MRS. MANNING: *Good Old Times (1549).

PRESCOTT: History of Philip II.

MOTLEY: The Rise of the Dutch Republic.

—— History of the United Netherlands.

YONGE: *The Chaplet of Pearls (France, 1555).

BARRETT: William the Silent (1533-1584).

BAIRD: Rise of the Huguenots.

SMILES: The Huguenots in France.

ABBOTT: HISTORY OF HENRY IV. OF FRANCE.

GUIZOT: History of France, vol. iv.

GOETHE: †Egmont (1568).

JAMES: *The Man-at-Arms (1572).

SOUTHEY: ‡St. Bartholomew's Day (1572).

MACAULAY: ‡Ivry (1590).

GOETHE: †Torquato Tasso (1590).

TROLLOPE: *Paul the Pope and Paul the Friar.

ROBSON:Life of Cardinal Richelieu (1585-1642).

JAMES: *Richelieu.

BULWER: *Richelieu.

MANZONI: *The Betrothed (1628).

GOETHE: ‡The Destruction of Magdeburg.

SCHILLER: †Wallenstein (1634).

TOPELIUS: *Times of Gustaf Adolf.

GARDINER: History of the Thirty Years' War.

SCHILLER: History of the Thirty Years' War.

MOTLEY: Life of John of Barneveld.

PARDOE: *Louis XIV. and the Court of France.

JAMES: Louis XIV.

GUIZOT: History of France, vol. v.

ABBOTT: HISTORY OF LOUIS

GOLDWIN SMITH: Three English Statesmen.

MACAULAY: ‡The Cavalier's March to London (1651).

MASSON: Life and Times of John Milton.

YONGE: *The Pigeon Pie; a Tale of Roundhead Times.

SHORTHOUSE: *John Inglesant.

JAMES: *The Cavalier (1651).

BUTLER: ‡Hudibras.

SCOTT: *Woodstock.

MARVELL: ‡Blake's Victory (1657).

ABBOTT: HISTORY OF CHARLES II.

DRYDEN: ‡Annus Mirabilis (1666).

BIRCHALL: England under the Stuarts.

FOX: Life of James II.

AINSWORTH: *James II.

JAMES: *Russell.

MACAULAY: History of England (1685-1702).

—— Essay on Sir William Temple.

AYTOUN: ‡The Widow of Glencoe (1692).

HALE: The Fall of the Stuarts.

MORRIS: The Age of Anne.

COXE: Memoirs of the Duke of Marlborough.

SCOTT: *Old Mortality.

—— *The Bride of Lammermoor.

DEFOE: *Memoirs of a Cavalier.

—— *History of the Great Plague in London.

ADDISON: The Spectator.

THACKERAY: *Henry Esmond.

BLACKMORE: *Lorna Doone.

ADDISON: *The Battle of Blenheim (1704).

PEPYS: Diary (1659-1703).

GREEN: History of the English People, book viii.

130

LECKY: History of England in the Eighteenth Century.

GREEN: History of the English People, book ix.

SCOTT: *Rob Roy (1715).

—— *The Heart of Mid-Lothian.

THACKERAY: Lectures on the Four Georges.

STEPHEN: History of English Thought in the Eighteenth Century.

MACAULAY: Essays on Lord Clive and Lord Chatham.

FROUDE: The English in Ireland in the XIV.

MANNING: *Idyl of the Alps.

BUNGENER: BOURDALOUE AND LOUIS XIV.

TOPELIUS: *Times of Battle and Rest.

MACAULAY: ‡Song of the Huguenots (1685).

BROWNING: Hervé Riel (1692).

ABBOTT: HISTORY OF PETER THE GREAT.

SCHUYLER: History of Peter the Great.

MAHON: War of the Spanish Succession.

MÜHLBACH: *Prince Eugene and his Times.

TOPELIUS: *Times of Charles XII.

VOLTAIRE: History of Charles XII.

MARTINEAU: *Messrs. Vandeput and Snoek (1695).

LADY JACKSON: The Old Régime (Louis XIV. and XV.).

MACAULAY: Essay on the War of the Succession in Spain.

TOPELIUS: *Times of Frederick I. (1721).

BUNGENER: LOUIS XV. AND HIS TIMES.

HELPS: Ivan de Biron (1740).

MACAULAY: Essay on Frederick the Great.

ABBOTT: HISTORY OF MARIE ANTOINETTE.

DAVIS: *Fontenoy (1745).

LONGMAN: Frederick the Great and the Seven Years' War.

CARLYLE: Life of Frederick the Great.

Eighteenth Century.
CAMPBELL: ‡Lochiel's Warning.
SCOTT: *Waverley (1745).
MOIR: ‡The Battle of Prestonpans (1745).
SMOLLETT: ‡The Tears of Scotland.
GOLDSMITH: *The Vicar of Wakefield.
SOUTHEY: Life and Times of John Wesley.
MRS. CHARLES: *Diary of Kitty Trevylyan.
MITFORD: *Our Village.
EDGEWORTH: *Castle Rackrent.
THACKERAY: *The Virginians (1775).
SCOTT: *Guy Mannering.
DICKENS: *Barnaby Rudge (1780).
MACAULAY: Essays on Warren Hastings, William Pitt, and Barère.
GOLDWIN SMITH: Three English Statesmen.
TREVELYAN: Early History of Charles James Fox.
WADE: Letters of Junius.
MORLEY: Edmund Burke, a Historical Sketch.
BLACKMORE: *The Maid of Sker.
GEORGE ELIOT: *Adam Bede.
COOPER: *Wing and Wing.
LEVER: *Charles O'Malley.
MRS. CHARLES: *Against the Stream.
THACKERAY: *Vanity Fair.

MAGINN: *Whitehall.
PALGRAVE: ‡Trafalgar (1805).
ROBERT BUCHANAN: †The Shadow of the Sword.
KINGSLEY: *Alton Locke.
DISRAELI: *Sybil.
SOUTHEY: ‡The Battle of Algiers (1815).
MCCARTHY: History of our own Times.
MARTINEAU: History of the Thirty Years' Peace.
CARLYLE: Latter-Day Pamphlets.
DISRAELI: *Lothair.
KINGLAKE: The Invasion of the Crimea.

YONGE: Life of Marie Antoinette.
MÜHLBACH: *Frederick the Great and his Family.
TOPELIUS: *Times of Linnæus.
GUIZOT: History of France, vol. vi.
TOPELIUS: *Times of Alchemy.
TAINE: The Ancient Régime.
ABBOTT: The French Revolution of 1789.
—— HISTORY OF THE EMPRESS JOSEPHINE.
—— HISTORY OF MADAME ROLAND.
—— HISTORY OF QUEEN HORTENSE.
ALISON: History of Europe (1789-1815), abridged by Gould.
131
TAINE: Origins of Contemporary France.
VAN LAUN: The French Revolutionary Epoch.
ADAMS: Democracy and Monarchy in France.
VICTOR HUGO: *Ninety-Three.
COLERIDGE: ‡Destruction of the Bastile.
RENAUD: ‡The Last Banquet.
ERCKMANN-CHATRIAN: *Year One of the Republic.
DICKENS: *A Tale of Two Cities.
BLACKMORE: *Alice Lorraine.
TROLLOPE: *La Vendée.
SAINTINE: *Picciola.
FRITZ REUTER: *In the Year Thirteen.
ERCKMANN-CHATRIAN: *The Conscript; The Invasion of France in 1814; and Waterloo.
BYRON: ‡The Battle of Waterloo.
MOORE: *The Fudge Family in Paris.
MARTINEAU: *French Wine and Politics.
VICTOR HUGO: *Les Misérables.
GUIZOT: France under Louis Philippe.
VICTOR HUGO: The History of a Crime.
BULWER: *The Parisians.

MURRAY: *The Member for Paris.

FORBES: The Franco-German War.

132

IV. AMERICAN HISTORY.

General Histories.

Bancroft: *History of the United States* (12 vols., from the discovery of America to the adoption of the Constitution).

Hildreth: *History of the United States* (6 vols., from the discovery of America to 1820).

Bryant and Gay: *History of the United States* (from the discovery to 1880).

Ridpath: *History of the United States.*

Higginson: YOUNG PEOPLE'S HISTORY OF THE UNITED STATES.

Aboriginal America.

Baldwin: Ancient America.

Donnelly: Atlantis.

Foster: Prehistoric Races of the United States.

Short: North Americans of Antiquity.

Ellis: The Red Man and the White Man.

H. H. Bancroft: Native Races of the Pacific States.

Bourke: The Snake Dance of the Moquis of Arizona.

The Period of the Discovery.

Irving: Columbus and his Companions.

Abbott: CHRISTOPHER COLUMBUS.

—— DISCOVERY OF AMERICA.

Towle: VASCO DA GAMA.

Helps: The Spanish Conquest of America (4 vols.).

Prescott: The Conquest of Mexico (3 vols.).

Abbott: HERNANDO CORTEZ.

Helps: Hernando Cortez.

Eggleston: MONTEZUMA.

Wallace: *The Fair God, or the Last of the 'Tzins.

133

Prescott: The Conquest of Peru (2 vols.).

Towle: PIZARRO.

—— MAGELLAN.

Irving: The Conquest of Florida by De Soto.

Abbott: DE SOTO.

Simms: *Vasconselos (1538).

Towle: DRAKE, THE SEA-KING OF DEVON.

—— SIR WALTER RALEGH.

Hale: Stories of Discovery.

Simms: *The Lily and the Totem (the story of the Huguenots at St. Augustine).

The Colonial Period.

Coffin: Old Times in the Colonies.

Simms: Life of John Smith.

Kingston: *The Settlers (1607).

Eggleston: POCAHONTAS.

Abbott: THE NORTHERN COLONIES.

—— Miles Standish.

Longfellow: ‡The Courtship of Miles Standish.

Mrs. Child: *The First Settlers of New England.

—— *Hobomok.

Cheney: *A Peep at the Pilgrims.

Clay: Annals of the Swedes on the Delaware.

Banvard: PIONEERS OF THE NEW WORLD.
J. G. Holland: *The Bay Path (1638).
Paulding: *Koningsmarke (a tale of the Swedes on the Delaware).
Arthur: CABINET HISTORY OF NEW YORK.
Abbott: PETER STUYVESANT.
Irving: *Knickerbocker's History of New York.
Abbott: KING PHILIP.
Markham: King Philip's War.
Cooper: *The Wept of Wish-ton-Wish (1675).
Palfrey: History of New England (4 vols.).
Hawthorne: *The Scarlet Letter.
134
Spofford: New England Legends.
Longfellow: ‡New England Tragedies.
Whittier: ‡Ballads of New England.
Hale: Stories of Adventure.
Abbott: CAPTAIN KIDD.
Banvard: Southern Explorers.
Abbott: THE SOUTHERN COLONIES.
Arthur: Cabinet History of Virginia.
Simms: *The Cassique of Kiawah (a story of the early settlement of South Carolina, 1684).
De Vere: Romance of American History.
Abbott: CHEVALIER DE LA SALLE.
Parkman: Discovery of the Great West.
—— The Jesuits in North America.
Sparks: Life of Father Marquette.
Shea: Discovery and Exploration of the Mississippi.
Parkman: Frontenac, and New France under Louis XIV.
Simms: *The Yemassee (1715).
Longfellow: ‡Evangeline.
Ladd: The Old French War.
Parkman: Wolfe and Montcalm.
—— The Conspiracy of Pontiac.
Paulding: *The Dutchman's Fireside.
Cooper: *The Pathfinder.
—— *The Last of the Mohicans.
Kennedy: *Swallow Barn.
Mrs. Stowe: *The Minister's Wooing.
Thackeray: *The Virginians.

The Period of the Revolution.

Abbott: THE WAR OF THE REVOLUTION.
—— GEORGE WASHINGTON.
Irving: Life of George Washington (5 vols.).
Headley: Washington and his Generals.
Longfellow: ‡Paul Revere's Ride.
135
Lowell: ‡Grandmother's Story of the Battle of Bunker Hill.
Coffin: THE BOYS OF '76.
Cooper: *The Spy.
—— *The Pilot.
Neal: *Seventy-Six.
Greene: Life of Nathanael Greene.
Abbott: LIFE OF BENJAMIN FRANKLIN.
Parton: Life of Benjamin Franklin.
Sparks: The Works of Benjamin Franklin.

—— Treason of Benedict Arnold.
Arnold: Life of Benedict Arnold.
Campbell: ‡Gertrude of Wyoming.
Mrs. Child: *The Rebels.
Paulding: *The Old Continentals.
—— *The Bulls and the Jonathans.
Simms: *Eutaw.
Kennedy: *Horse-Shoe Robinson.
Grace Greenwood: *The Forest Tragedy.
Lossing: Field Book of the Revolution.
Carrington: Battles of the Revolution.
Wirt: The Life of Patrick Henry.
Dwight: Lives of the Signers.
Magoon: Orators of the American Revolution.
Greene: Historical View of the American Revolution.

From the Close of the Revolution.

McMaster: History of the People of the United States from the Revolution to the Civil War.
Frothingham: Rise of the Republic in the United States.
Curtis: History of the Constitution.
Von Holst: Constitutional History of the United States.
Nordhoff: POLITICS FOR YOUNG AMERICANS.
136
Coffin: BUILDING OF THE NATION.
Lodge: Life of Alexander Hamilton.
Parton: Life of John Adams.
—— Life of Jefferson.
Abbott: LIFE OF DANIEL BOONE.
John Esten Cooke: *Leatherstocking and Silk (1800).
Cable: *The Grandissimes.
Cooper: *The Prairie.
Simms: *Beauchampe, or the Kentucky Tragedy.
Parton: Life of Aaron Burr.
Hale: *Philip Nolan's Friends.
—— *The Man without a Country.
Pioneer Life in the West.
Lewis and Clarke's Journey across the Rocky Mountains.
Irving: Astoria.
—— Adventures of Captain Bonneville.
Eggleston: Brant and Red Jacket.
Johnson: The War of 1812.
Lossing: Field Book of the War of 1812.
Iron: *The Double Hero.
Gleig: *The Subaltern.
Cooper: History of the American Navy.
Rives: Life of James Madison.
Gilman: Life of James Monroe.
Morse: Life of J. Q. Adams.
Parton: Life of Andrew Jackson.
Curtis: Life of Daniel Webster.
Whipple: Webster's Best Speeches.
Schmucker: Life and Times of Henry Clay.
Ripley: The War with Mexico.
Kendall: The Santa Fé Expedition.
Wilson: History of the Rise and Fall of the Slave Power in America.
137

King: The Great South.
Olmsted: The Sea-Board Slave States.
Mrs. Stowe: *Uncle Tom's Cabin.
Hildreth: *The White Slave.
Whittier: ‡Voices of Freedom.
Greeley: The American Conflict.
Lossing: The Civil War in the United States.
Draper: History of the American Civil War.
Stephens: Constitutional History of the War between the States (Southern view).
Harper's Pictorial History of the Great Rebellion.
YOUNG FOLKS' HISTORY OF THE REBELLION.
Coffin: THE BOYS OF '61.
—— *WINNING HIS WAY.
Hale: Stories of War.
Richardson: Field, Dungeon, and Escape.
Swinton: Twelve Decisive Battles of the War.
Cooke: Life of General Lee.
Whittier: ‡In War Time.
Lester: Our First Hundred Years.
Lossing: The American Centenary.
Tourgee: *A Fool's Errand.
—— *Bricks without Straw.
Headley: HEROES OF THE REBELLION (6 vols.).

138

CHAPTER VIII.

Courses of Reading in Geography and Natural History

EOGRAPHY is learned best by the careful reading of books of travel. Pupils would derive infinitely more knowledge by the use, under judicious instructors, of a library of this sort, than by years of drudging through those masses of inanity known as School Geographies. The following list is designed chiefly to aid teachers in the selection of books suitable for geographical study at school, and to assist private readers in the choice of useful and entertaining works on the various subjects of interest in our own and foreign countries.

A good atlas is the first desideratum, and is an indispensable auxiliary to the course of reading here indicated. Rand, McNally, & Co.'s Atlas is one of the latest publications, and perhaps the most accurate and complete139 in the market. Among other very good works of this kind we may mention Gray's, Johnson's, Colton's, and Zell's, any one of which will answer all the ordinary purposes of the reader. When no complete work is available, the maps in the larger school geographies will render very fair service.

The World.

Coffin: OUR NEW WAY ROUND THE WORLD.
Curtis: Dottings round the Circle.
Dana: TWO YEARS BEFORE THE MAST.
Hall: DRIFTING ROUND THE WORLD.
Gerstacker: A Journey round the World.
Prime: Around the World.
Pumpelly: Across America and Asia.
Smiles: A BOY'S JOURNEY ROUND THE WORLD.
Nordhoff: MAN-OF-WAR LIFE.
Knox: THE YOUNG NIMRODS AROUND THE WORLD.
Hale: STORIES OF THE SEA, TOLD BY SAILORS.
Verne: FAMOUS TRAVELS AND TRAVELLERS.
—— THE GREAT NAVIGATORS.
—— THE EXPLORERS OF THE NINETEENTH CENTURY.
Figuier: The Ocean World.
—— The Insect World.
Mrs. Brassey: Voyage in the Sunbeam.
Ainsworth: All round the World.
Harper: WHAT DARWIN SAW.
Humboldt: Cosmos.

North America.

Butterworth: ZIGZAG JOURNEYS IN THE OCCIDENT.
Knox: THE YOUNG NIMRODS IN NORTH AMERICA.
140
Rideing: BOYS IN THE MOUNTAINS.
Hawthorne: AMERICAN NIGHTS' ENTERTAINMENT.
Ingersoll: FRIENDS WORTH KNOWING; Glimpses of American Natural History.
Hale: STORIES OF DISCOVERY.
Say: Insects of North America.
Drake: Nooks and Corners of the New England Coast.
Flagg: The Woods and By-Ways of New England.
Nordhoff: *Cape Cod and all along Shore.
Thoreau: The Maine Woods.
—— A Week on the Concord.
—— Cape Cod.
—— Excursions in Field and Forest.
Samuels: The Birds of New England.
Scudder: THE BODLEYS AFOOT.
Drake: AROUND THE HUB; A Boy's Book about Boston.
Longfellow: Poems of Places, vol. xxvi.

Murray: Adventures in the Wilderness; or, Camp Life in the Adirondacks.
Warner: The Adirondacks Verified.
Bromfield: Picturesque Journeys in America.
Jordan: Vertebrates of the Northern States.
Appleton: Picturesque America.
—— Our Native Land.
Howells: *Their Wedding Journey.
Longfellow: Poems of Places, vol. xxvii.
King: The Great South.
Olmsted: The Sea-Board Slave States.
Baldwin: The Flush Times of Alabama and Mississippi.
Pollard: The Virginia Tourist.141 Twain: Life on the Mississippi.
Lanier: Florida; its Scenery.
Porte Crayon: Virginia Illustrated.
Longfellow: Poems of Places, vol. xxviii.
Lewis and Clarke's Expedition across the Rocky Mountains.
Irving: Astoria.
—— Adventures of Captain Bonneville.
—— A Tour on the Prairies.
Meline: Two Thousand Miles on Horseback.
Richardson: Beyond the Mississippi.
Browne: Crusoe's Island.
Nordhoff: Northern California.
Taylor: Eldorado.
Codman: The Round Trip.
Bird: A Lady's Life in the Rocky Mountains.
Ingersoll: Knocking round the Rockies.
Cozzens: The Marvellous Country; or, Three Years in Arizona and New Mexico.
Browne: The Apache Country.
Taylor: Colorado; A Summer Trip.
Richardson: Wonders of the Yellowstone.
Longfellow: Poems of Places, vol. xxix.
Robinson: The Great Fur Land.
Butler: The Great Lone Land.
—— The Wild North Land.
Hartwig: The Polar World.
Hayes: The Land of Desolation.
Blake: Arctic Experiences.
Nourse: American Explorations in the Ice Zones.
Burton: Ultima Thule.
Stephens: OFF TO THE GEYSERS.
Haven: Our Next-Door Neighbor.
Wilson: Mexico; its Peasants and Priests.
142
Ruxton: Adventures in Mexico.
Stephens: Travels in Yucatan.
—— Travels in Central America.
Squier: The States of Central America.
Ober: *THE SILVER CITY.
Kingsley: A Christmas in the West Indies.
Hurlbert: Gan Eden; or, Pictures of Cuba.
Dana: To Cuba and Back.

South America.

Holton: New Granada.
Orton: The Andes and Amazon.
Agassiz: Journey in Brazil.

Ewbank: Life in Brazil.
Fletcher: Brazil and the Brazilians.
Bishop: A THOUSAND MILES' WALK ACROSS SOUTH AMERICA.
Marcoy: Travels across South America.
Hassaurek: Four Years among Spanish Americans.
Squier: Peru.
Orton: *THE SECRET OF THE ANDES.
Stephens: ON THE AMAZONS.
Dixie: Across Patagonia.
Reid: *THE LAND OF FIRE.
Longfellow: Poems of Places, vol. xxx.

Europe.

Butterworth: ZIGZAG JOURNEYS IN EUROPE.
Champney: THREE VASSAR GIRLS ABROAD.
Scudder: THE ENGLISH BODLEY FAMILY.
Hawthorne: Our Old Home.
Taine: Notes on England.
Escott: England.
Miller: First Impressions of England and its People.
Emerson: English Traits.
143
Hoppin: Old England; Its Scenery, Art, and People.
Abbott: A Summer in Scotland.
Miller: Scenes and Legends of the North of Scotland.
White: Natural History of Selborne.
Longfellow: Poems of Places, vols. i.-v.
Longfellow: Outre Mer.
Taylor: Views Afoot.
Macquoid: Through Normandy.
Hamerton: Round My House.
Hale: A FAMILY FLIGHT THROUGH FRANCE, GERMANY, AND SWITZERLAND.
Walworth: THE OLD WORLD SEEN THROUGH YOUNG EYES.
Bulwer: France, Literary, Social, and Political.
Longfellow: Poems of Places, vols. vi.-x.
Taine: Tour through the Pyrenees.
Hale: A FAMILY FLIGHT THROUGH SPAIN.
De Amicis: Spain and the Spaniards.
Bodfish: Through Spain on Donkey-Back.
Hare: Wanderings in Spain.
Hay: Castilian Days.
Irving: The Alhambra.
—— Spanish Papers.
Andersen: Pictures of Travel.
Latouche: Travels in Portugal.
Longfellow: Poems of Places, vols. xiv., xv.
Butterworth: ZIGZAG JOURNEYS IN CLASSIC LANDS.
Browne: Yusef; Travels on the Shores of the Mediterranean.
Eustis: Classical Tour through Italy.
Dickens: Pictures from Italy.
Hare: Cities of Northern and Central Italy.
—— Days near Rome.
144
Hawthorne: English and Italian Notes.
Howells: Italian Journeys.
—— Venetian Life.
Taine: Italy (Florence and Venice).

—— Italy (Rome and Naples).
Di Cesnola: Cyprus.
Longfellow: Poems of Places, vols. xi.-xiii.
Stephens: Travels in Greece and Turkey.
Mahaffy: Rambles and Studies in Greece.
Baird: Modern Greece.
Townsend: A Cruise in the Bosphorus.
De Amicis: Constantinople.
Gautier: Constantinople.
Longfellow: Poems of Places, vol. xix.
Waring: Tyrol and the Skirt of the Alps.
Whymper: Scrambles among the Alps.
Taylor: The By-Ways of Europe.
Hugo: Tour on the Rhine.
Browne: An American Family in Germany.
Hawthorne: Saxon Studies.
Hugo: Home-Life in Germany.
Baring-Gould: Germany, Past and Present.
De Amicis: Holland.
Scudder: THE BODLEYS IN HOLLAND.
Dodge: *HANS BRINKER, OR THE SILVER SKATES.
Havard: Picturesque Holland.
Butterworth: ZIGZAG JOURNEYS IN NORTHERN LANDS.
Taylor: Northern Europe.
Browne: Land of Thor.
Du Chaillu: The Land of the Midnight Sun.
Andersen: Pictures of Travel in Sweden.
MacGregor: Rob Roy on the Baltic.
Longfellow: Poems of Places, vols. xvii., xviii.
145
Butterworth: ZIGZAG JOURNEYS IN THE ORIENT.
Gautier: A Winter in Russia.
Wallace: Russia.
Richardson: Ralph's Year in Russia.
Morley: Sketches of Russian Life.
Dixon: Free Russia.

Asia.

Kennan: Tent Life in Siberia.
McGahan: Campaigning on the Oxus.
Burnaby: A Ride to Khiva.
Schuyler: Turkistan.
Taylor: Central Asia.
Arnold: Through Persia by Caravan.
Stack: Six Months in Persia.
Vámbéry: Travels in Central Asia.
O'Donovan: The Merv Oasis.
Curtis: The Howadji in Syria.
Kinglake: Eöthen.
MacGregor: Rob Roy on the Jordan.
Prime: Tent Life in the Holy Land.
Taylor: Travels in Arabia.
Blunt: The Bedouin Tribes.
Keane: Six Months in Mecca.
Baker: Rifle and Hound in Ceylon.
Butler: The Land of the Vedas.
French: OUR BOYS IN INDIA.

Knox: THE BOY TRAVELLERS IN INDIA AND CEYLON.
—— THE BOY TRAVELLERS IN SIAM AND JAVA.
Vincent: The Land of the White Elephant.
Leonowens: An English Governess at the Siamese Court.
Kingston: *IN EASTERN SEAS.
146
Wilson: The Abode of Snow.
Markham: Thibet.
Gordon: The Roof of the World.
Williams: The Middle Kingdom.
Taylor: India, China, and Japan.
French: OUR BOYS IN CHINA.
Eden: China, Japan, and India.
Oppert: Corea.
Knox: THE BOY TRAVELLERS IN JAPAN AND CHINA.
Miller: LITTLE PEOPLE OF ASIA.
—— CHILD LIFE IN JAPAN.
Greey: THE WONDERFUL CITY OF TOKIO.
—— THE BEAR WORSHIPPERS.
Griffis: The Mikado's Empire.
Bird: Unbeaten Tracks in Japan.
Longfellow: Poems of Places, vols. xxi.-xxiii.

Africa.

Hale: A FAMILY FLIGHT OVER EGYPT AND SYRIA.
Knox: THE BOY TRAVELLERS IN EGYPT.
—— THE BOY TRAVELLERS IN CENTRAL AFRICA.
McCabe: OUR YOUNG FOLKS IN AFRICA.
Du Chaillu: WILD LIFE UNDER THE EQUATOR.
—— THE COUNTRY OF THE DWARFS.
Baker: *CAST UP BY THE SEA.
Stanley: *MY KALULU.
Baker: Ismailia.
—— Albert N'Yanza.
Speke: Journal of the Discovery of the Source of the Nile.
Edwards: A Thousand Miles up the Nile.
Taylor: Central Africa.
Schweinfurth: The Heart of Africa.
147
Livingstone: Last Journals.
Stanley: How I found Livingstone.
—— Through the Dark Continent.
Du Chaillu: Explorations in Central Africa.
—— Journey to Ashango Land.
Anderson: Southwestern Africa.
Livingstone: South Africa.
Cumming: Hunter's Life in South Africa.
MacLeod: Madagascar and its People.
Longfellow: Poems of Places, vol. xxiv.

Australia and the Pacific.

Grant: Bush Life in Australia.
Cook: Voyages round the World.
Gironierre: Twenty Years in the Philippine Islands.
Nordhoff: Stories of the Island World.
Cheever: The Island World of the Pacific.
Lamont: Wild Life among the Pacific Islanders.
Bird: Six Months among the Sandwich Islands.

Dana: Corals and Coral Islands.

148

CHAPTER IX.

Philosophy and Religion.

A LITTLE philosophy inclineth a man's mind to atheism, but depth in philosophy bringeth men's minds about to religion.—BACON.

HE books which help you most are those which make you think the most," says Theodore Parker. "The hardest way of learning is by easy reading; every man that tries it finds it so."

And apropos of this, I present the following list of books recommended by Dr. John Brown as suitable for the reading of young medical students. Yet not only medical students, but students of other special subjects, and teachers as well, will find it profitable to dig into and through, to "energize upon" and master, such books as these—

149

1. Arnauld's Port Royal Logic; translated by T. S. Baynes.
2. Thomson's Outlines of the Necessary Laws of Thought.
3. Descartes on the Method of Rightly Conducting the Reason and Seeking Truth in the Sciences.
4. Coleridge's Essay on Method.
5. Whately's Logic and Rhetoric (new and cheap edition).
6. Mill's Logic (new and cheap edition).
7. Dugald Stewart's Outlines.
8. Sir John Herschel's Preliminary Dissertation.
9. Isaac Taylor's Elements of Thought.
10. Sir William Hamilton's edition of Reid: Dissertations and Lectures.
11. Professor Fraser's Rational Philosophy.
12. Locke on the Conduct of the Understanding.

"Taking up a book like Arnauld, and reading a chapter of his lively, manly sense," says Rab's friend, "is like throwing your manuals, and scalpels, and microscopes, and natural (most unnatural) orders out of your hand and head, and taking a game with the Grange Club, or a run to the top of Arthur Seat. Exertion quickens your pulse, expands your lungs, makes your blood warmer and redder, fills your mouth with the pure waters of relish, strengthens and supples your legs; and though on your way to the top you may encounter rocks, and baffling débris, and gusts of fierce winds rushing out upon you from behind150 corners, just as you will find, in Arnauld and all truly serious and honest books of the kind, difficulties and puzzles, winds of doctrine, and deceitful mists, still you are rewarded at the top by the wide view. You see, as from a tower, the end of all. You look into the perfections and relations of things; you see the clouds, the bright lights, and the everlasting hills on the horizon. You come down the hill a happier, a better, and a hungrier man, and of a better mind. But, as we said, you must eat the book,—you must crush it, and cut it with your teeth, and swallow it; just as you must walk up, and not be carried up, the hill, much less imagine you are there, or look upon a picture of what you would see were you up, however accurately or artistically done; no,—you yourself must *do* both."

The same may be said of all books that are the most truly helpful to us, and mind-lifting. It is the hard reading that profits most, provided, always, that due care be taken to digest that which is read. Yet I would not recommend the same strong diet or the same severe exercise to every person, or even to any considerable proportion of readers. One man may be a palm, as says Dr. Collyer, and another a pine; that which is wisdom to the151one may be incomprehensible folly to the other. But those whose mental constitutions are sufficiently vigorous to digest and assimilate the food which the philosophers offer, may find comfort and health, not only in the works above recommended, but in the following—

Plato's Works: Jowett's translation.

G. H. Lewes: A Chapter from Aristotle.

Lord Bacon: Novum Organum.

Butler: Analogy of Religion, Natural and Revealed.

Hume: A Treatise on Human Nature.

Hamilton: Discussions on Philosophy and Literature.

Mill: Examination of Hamilton's Philosophy.
Lewes: Problems of Life and Mind.
Cousin: Lectures on the True, the Beautiful, and the Good.
Martineau: The Positive Philosophy of Auguste Comte.
Mill: Comte and Positivism.
Mahaffy: Kant's Critical Philosophy for English Readers.
Fichte: The Science of Knowledge.
Meiklejohn: Kant's Critique of the Pure Reason (published in Bohn's Philosophical Library).
Spencer: First Principles of Philosophy.
Bowen: Essays on Speculative Philosophy.
Porter: Elements of Intellectual Science.
—— The Human Intellect.
McCosh: Intuitions of the Mind.
—— System of Logic.
Fiske: Outlines of Cosmic Philosophy.
Everett: Science of Thought.
152
Wallace: The Logic of Hegel.
Hegel: The Philosophy of History (translated by J. Sibree, in Bohn's Philosophical Library).
Schopenhauer: Select Essays of Arthur Schopenhauer (translated by Droppers and Dachsel).
Lewes: Biographical History of Philosophy.
Morell: An Historical and Critical View of the Speculative Philosophy of Europe in the Nineteenth Century.
Ueberweg: History of Philosophy.
Masson: Recent British Philosophy.
Lecky: History of European Morals.
—— History of Rationalism in Europe.
Draper: History of the Intellectual Development of Europe.
To the foregoing list the following may be added—
Plutarch's Morals (translated by Goodwin).
Thoughts of Marcus Aurelius Antoninus (in the "Wisdom Series").
Selections from Fénelon.
Burton's Anatomy of Melancholy.
Sydney Smith's Sketches of Moral Philosophy.
Watts on the Mind.
Taine on Intelligence.

A course of reading which shall include any number of the works here mentioned will be no child's play; it will involve the severest exercise of the thinking powers, but it will enable you "to look into the perfections and relations of things, and to see the clouds, the bright lights, and the everlasting hills on the153 horizon." The reading of such books is like the training of a gymnast; it will lead to the healthy development of the parts most skillfully exercised, but the strength of him who exercises should never be too severely tested. Would you prefer a lighter course of reading, but one which will probably lead you into pleasanter paths of contemplation and reflection, and finally open up to your view a prospect equally boundless and grand? Allow me to suggest the following, which is neither philosophical nor religious, in the strictest acceptation of these terms, but which leads us to an acquaintance with that which is best in both.

We shall begin with the Bible, and throughout the course we shall make that book our grand rallying-point. "Read the Bible reverently and attentively," says Sir Matthew Hale; "set your heart upon it, and lay it up in your memory, and make it the direction of your life: it will make you a wise and good man." From the reverential reading of the Bible, which to most of us is rather an act of religious duty than of intellectual effort, we turn to the great masterpieces of antiquity. In the Phædo and the Apology and Crito of Plato, we find the ripest thoughts of the world's154 greatest thinker; then we turn to Aristotle's Ethics, and, afterwards, we compare the doctrines of the Greek philosophers with the Teachings of Confucius and of Mencius.[22] If we have supplemented these readings with the proper acquaintance with ancient history, we shall now be ready to understand the great poems of antiquity, and to read them in a light different from that which we have hitherto known. We read the Iliad, and the Odyssey, and the Greek tragedians; then the old Indian epics, Arnold's "The Light of Asia," and Swamy's "Dialogues and Discourses of Gotama Buddha." Descending now to more modern times,—for we would not make this course a long one,—we turn again to our Bible, and thoroughly acquaint ourselves with "the unsurpassedly simple, loving, perfect idyls of the life and death of Christ," as we find them in the New Testament. After this, we shall obtain more exalted ideas of the brotherhood of the human race and the "hope of the nations," if we spend some time in the study of the majestic expressions of the universal conscience found in such works as the "Vishnu Sarma" of the Hindoos, the "Gulistan" of Saadi, the "Sentences" 155of Epictetus, and the "Thoughts" of Marcus Aurelius Antoninus. Then, to get at the poetic interpretation of the teachings of Mohammed, we read the "Pearls of Faith; or, Islam's Rosary," and Lane Poole's "Selections from the Koran." Returning to the study of Christian ethics and poetry, we take up the "Confessions of Saint Augustine," and the "Discourse" of Saint Bernard, and then the "Imitation of Christ," by Thomas à Kempis. We read Milton's "Paradise Lost" again, and Bunyan's "Pilgrim's Progress;" and we enjoy the wealth of imagery in Jeremy Taylor's "Holy Living and Holy Dying." Holy George Herbert's "Sacred Poems and Private Ejaculations" claim our attention for a time, and then we take up Pascal's "Thoughts," and selections from Fénelon's "Telemachus" and "Dialogues of the Dead." Finally, we read Wordsworth's "Excursion," and Keble's "Christian Year," and return after all to a further perusal of the Bible and the poems of antiquity.

You may say that this course is rather fragmentary, and so it is; but it differs from the other courses which I have indicated, in that it is undertaken as a heart-work rather than a head-work. Unlike the course just preceding,156 it has to do with our emotional and devotional natures rather than with our highest powers of thinking and reasoning. With few exceptions only, the books here mentioned are voices out of the past, speaking to us of the human soul's belief and experience in different ages of the world and under different dispensations. "I suppose," says George Eliot, speaking of the "Imitation of Christ,"—"I suppose that is the reason why the small old-fashioned book, for which you need only pay sixpence at a book-stall, works miracles to this day, turning bitter waters into sweetness; while expensive sermons and treatises, newly issued, leave all things as they were before. It was written down by a hand that waited for the heart's prompting; it is the chronicle of a solitary, hidden anguish, struggle, trust, and triumph,—not written on velvet cushions to teach endurance to those who are treading with bleeding feet on the stones. And so it remains to all time a lasting record of human needs and human consolations; the voice of a brother who, ages ago, felt and suffered and renounced,—in the cloister, perhaps with serge gown and tonsured head, with much chanting and long fasts, and with a fashion of speech different from ours,—but under the157 same silent far-off heavens, and with the same passionate desires, the same strivings, the same failures, the same weariness."

Writing of works like these, Emerson says: "Their communications are not to be given or taken with the lips and the end of the tongue, but out of the glow of the cheek, and with the throbbing heart.... These are the Scriptures which the missionary might well carry over prairie, desert, and ocean, to Siberia, Japan, Timbuctoo. Yet he will find that the spirit which is in them journeys faster than he, and greets him on his arrival,—was there long before him. The missionary must be carried by it, and find it there, or he goes in vain. Is there any geography in these things? We call them Asiatic, we call them primeval; but perhaps that is only optical, for Nature is always equal to herself, and there are as good eyes and ears now in the planet as ever were. Only these ejaculations of the soul are uttered one or a few at a time, at long intervals, and it takes millenniums to make a Bible."

We are brought now naturally to the subject of Theological Literature. The number of books in this department is very great, and there are wide differences of opinion with158 regard to the merits of many of the best-known works. Without attempting to select always the best, I shall name only a sufficient number of books necessary for the use of such non-professional readers as may desire to acquire a moderate knowledge of the commonly accepted theological doctrines—

McClintock and Strong's Cyclopædia of Biblical, Theological, and Ecclesiastical Literature (10 vols.).

Smith's Dictionary of the Bible.

Young's Analytical Concordance to the Bible.

Barrow's Sacred Geography and Antiquities.

Dean Stanley's Sinai and Palestine in connection with their History.

Clark's Bible Atlas, with Maps and Plans.

Bissel's Historic Origin of the Bible.

Lange's Commentary on the Holy Scriptures.

Alford's The Greek Testament; and The New Testament for English Readers.

Oehler's Theology of the Old Testament.

Weiss's Biblical Theology of the New Testament.

Geikie's Hours with the Bible.

Lenormant's The Beginnings of History, according to the Bible and the Traditions of Oriental Peoples.

Dean Stanley's Lectures on the History of the Jewish Church.

Geikie's Life and Works of Christ.

Farrar's Life of Christ.

Farrar's Life and Work of St. Paul.

Conybeare and Howson's Life and Epistles of St. Paul.

Schaff's History of the Christian Church.

Dean Milman's History of Latin Christianity (8 vols.).

159

Dean Stanley's Lectures on the History of the Eastern Church.

Maurice's Religions of the World.

James Freeman Clarke's Ten Great Religions.

Moffatt's Comparative History of Religions.

Trench's Lectures on Mediæval Church History.

Ullman's Reformers before the Reformation.

Fisher's History of the Reformation.

Ranke's History of the Popes during the Sixteenth and Seventeenth Centuries.

Griesinger's History of the Jesuits.

Baird's Rise and Progress of the Huguenots in France.

Stevens's History of Methodism.

Tyerman's Life and Times of John Wesley.

Hagenbach's History of Christian Doctrines (translated by C. W. Buch).

Fisher's Faith and Rationalism.

McCosh's Christianity and Positivism.

Farrar's Critical History of Free Thought in reference to the Christian Religion.

Smith's Faith and Philosophy.

Calderwood's Relations of Science and Religion.

Max Müller's Science of Religion.

Christlieb's Counteracting Modern Infidelity.

Trench's Shipwrecks of Faith.

Walker's Philosophy of the Plan of Salvation.

Smyth's Old Faiths in New Light.

Brooks's Yale Lectures on Preaching.

Dorner's System of Christian Doctrine.

Goulburn's Thoughts on Personal Religion.

Richard Baxter, speaking of this class of books, says: "Such books have the advantage in many other respects: you may read an160 able preacher when you have but a mean one to hear. Every congregation cannot hear the most judicious or powerful preachers; but every single person may read the books of the most powerful and judicious. Preachers may be silenced or banished, when books may be at hand; books may be kept at a smaller charge than preachers: we may choose books which treat of that very subject which we desire to hear of. Books we may have at hand every day and hour, when we can have sermons but seldom, and at set times. If sermons be forgotten, they are gone. But a book we may read over and over until we remember it; and if we forget it, may again peruse it at our pleasure or at our leisure."

161

CHAPTER X.

Political Economy and the Science of Government.

THIS is that noble Science of Politics, which is equally removed from the barren theories of the utilitarian sophists, and from the petty craft, so often mistaken for statesmanship by minds grown narrow in habits of intrigue, jobbing, and official etiquette,—which of all sciences is the most important to the welfare of nations,—which of all sciences most tends to expand and invigorate the mind,—which draws nutriment and ornament from every part of philosophy and literature, and dispenses in return nutriment and ornament to all.—MACAULAY.

O the student of Political Economy and the Science of Government I offer the following lists of books, embracing the best works on the various subjects connected with this study. The classification has been made solely with reference to the subject-matter, without any attempt to indicate the order in which the books are to be studied,—as this would be impossible.

162

Constitutional History, etc.

Freeman: Growth of the English Constitution.

Creasy: Rise and Progress of the English Constitution.

Stubbs: Constitutional History of England.

Hallam: Constitutional History of England (1485-1759).

Curtis: History of the Constitution of the United States.

Von Holst: Constitutional History of the United States.

De Tocqueville: Democracy in the United States.

Townsend: ANALYSIS OF CIVIL GOVERNMENT.

Nordhoff: POLITICS FOR YOUNG AMERICANS.

Andrews: Manual of the United States Constitution.

Mulford: The Nation.

Story: Familiar Exposition of the United States Constitution.

Bancroft: History of the United States (vol. xi.).

Amos: The Science of Politics.

General Works on Political Economy.

Perry: AN INTRODUCTION TO POLITICAL ECONOMY.

Jevons: A PRIMER OF POLITICAL ECONOMY.

Fawcett: A MANUAL OF POLITICAL ECONOMY.

John Stuart Mill: Principles of Political Economy (People's edition).

Cairnes: Some Leading Principles of Political Economy Newly Expounded.

Walker: The Elements of Political Economy.

Perry: Elements of Political Economy.

Bastiat: Essays on Political Economy.

Bowen: American Political Economy.

Mason and Lalor: Primer of Political Economy.

163

On Population.

Malthus: The Principles of Population.

Mr. Malthus's doctrines are opposed in the following works—

Godwin: On Population (1820).

Sadler: The Law of Population (1830).

Alison: The Principles of Population, and their Connection with Human Happiness (1840).

Doubleday: The True Law of Population shown to be connected with the Food of the People (1854).

Herbert Spencer: The Principles of Biology (vol. ii.).

Rickards: Population and Capital (1854).

Greg: Enigmas of Life (1872).

The Malthusian doctrine is supported wholly or in part by—

Macaulay, in his Essay on Sadler's Law of Population;

Rev. Thomas Chalmers, in Political Economy in connection with the Moral State and Moral Prospects of Society;

David Ricardo, in Principles of Political Economy; and some other writers. See, also, Roscher's Political Economy.

On Wealth and Currency.

Adam Smith: An Inquiry into the Nature and Causes of Wealth.

Probably the most important book that has ever been written, and certainly the most valuable contribution ever made by a single man towards establishing the principles on which government should be based.—H. T. BUCKLE.

164

Jevons: Money and the Mechanism of Exchange.

A. Walker: The Science of Wealth.

F. A. Walker: Money.

Bagehot: Lombard Street; a Description of the Money Market.

Bonamy Price: Principles of Currency.

—— Currency and Banking.

Chevalier: Essay on the Probable Fall in the Value of Gold (translated by Cobden).

Ricardo: Proposals for an Economical Currency.

Poor: Money; its Laws and History.

McCulloch: On Metallic and Paper Money, and Banks.

Newcomb: The A B C of Finance.

Wells: Robinson Crusoe's Money.

Harvey: Paper Money, the Money of Civilization.

Sumner: History of American Currency.

Maclaren: History of the Currency.

Linderman: Money and Legal Tender of the United States.

Bolles: Financial History of the United States, from 1789 to 1860.

On Banking.

Macleod: The Elements of Banking.

—— Theory and Practice of Banking.

Bonamy Price: Currency and Banking.

Gibbons: The Banks of New York.

Atkinson: What is a Bank?

Gilbart: Principles and Practice of Banking.

Bagehot: Lombard Street.

Morse: Treatise on the Laws relating to Banks and Banking.

On Labor and Wages.

Henry George: Progress and Poverty.

Mallock: Property and Progress.

165

Walker: Wages and the Wages Class.

Brassey: Work and Wages.

Jevons: The State in relation to Labor.

Jervis: Labor and Capital.

Thornton: On Labor; its Wrongful Claims and Rightful Dues.

Wright: A Practical Treatise on Labor.

Young: Labor in Europe and America.

Bolles: Conflict of Labor and Capital.

About: Hand-Book of Social Economy.

On Socialism and Co-operation.

Nordhoff: Communistic Societies of the United States.

Noyes: History of American Socialism.

Ely: French and German Socialism in Modern Times.

Holyoake: History of Co-operation.

Woolsey: Socialism.

Barnard: Co-operation as a Business.

The student of socialism will doubtless be interested in reading some of the philosophical fictions and other works, written in various ages, describing fanciful or ideal communities and governments. The following are the best—

Plato's Republic.

Sir Thomas More's Utopia.

Bacon's New Atlantis.

Hall's *Mundus Alter et Idem.*

Harrington's Oceana.

Defoe's Essay on Projects.

166

Disraeli's Coningsby, or the New Generation.

Bulwer's The Coming Race.

On Taxation and Pauperism.

Peto: Taxation; its Levy and Expenditure.

Cobden Club Essay,—On Local Government and Taxation.

Encyclopædia Britannica: The Article on Taxation.

Fawcett: Pauperism; its Causes and Remedies.

Sir George Nicholl: Histories of the English, Scotch, and Irish Poor Laws.

Lecky: History of European Morals (vol. ii.).

On the Tariff Question.

The following works favor, more or less strongly, the doctrine of Free Trade—

Adam Smith: On the Wealth of Nations.

Walter: What is Free Trade?

Sumner: Lectures on the History of Protection in the United States.

Mongredien: History of the Free-Trade Movement.

Grosvenor: Does Protection Protect?

Bastiat: Sophisms of Protection.

Fawcett: Free Trade and Protection.

Butts: Protection and Free Trade.

The following are the most important works favoring Protection—

Horace Greeley: The Science of Political Economy.

E. Peshine Smith: A Manual of Political Economy.

R. E. Thompson: Social Science and National Economy.

H. C. Carey: Principles of Social Science.

Byles: Sophisms of Free Trade.

167

Works of Reference.

McCulloch: Literature of Political Economy.

Macleod: A Dictionary of Political Economy, Biographical, Historical, and Practical.

Lalor: Cyclopædia of Political Science and Political Economy.

McCulloch: Dictionary of Commerce.

Tooke: History of Prices, 1793 to 1856.

Rogers: History of Agriculture and Prices in England.

168

CHAPTER XI.

On the Practical Study of English Literature.

THE ocean of literature is without limit. How then shall we be able to perform a voyage, even to a moderate distance, if we waste our time in dalliance on the shore? Our only hope is in exertion. Let our only reward be that of industry.—RINGELBERGIUS.

HE student of English literature has indeed embarked upon a limitless ocean. A lifetime of study will serve only to make him acquainted with parts of that great expanse which lies open before him. He should pursue his explorations earnestly, and with the inquiring spirit of a true discoverer. His thirst for knowledge should be unquenchable; he should long always for that mind food which brings the right kind of mind growth. He should not rest satisfied with merely superficial attainments, but should strive for that thoroughness169 of knowledge without which there can be neither excellence nor enjoyment.

English literature is not to be learned from manuals. They are only helps,—charts, buoys, light-houses, if you will call them so; or they serve to you the purposes of guide-books. What do you think of the would-be tourist who stays at home and studies his Baedeker with the foolish thought that he is actually seeing the countries which the book describes? And yet I have known students, and not a few teachers, do a thing equally as foolish. With a Morley, or a Shaw, or even a Brooke in their hands, and a few names and dates at their tongues' ends, they imagine themselves viewing the great ocean of literature, ploughing its surface and exploring its depths, when in reality they are only wasting their time "in dalliance on the shore."

English literature does not consist in a mere array of names and dates and short biographical sketches of men who have written books. Biography is biography; literature "is a record of the best thoughts." But the former is frequently studied in place of the latter. "For once that we take down our Milton, and read a book of that 'voice,' as Wordsworth says, 'whose sound is like the sea,'170 we take up fifty times a magazine with something about Milton, or about Milton's grandmother, or a book stuffed with curious facts about the houses in which he lived, and the juvenile ailments of his first wife."[23] Instead of becoming acquainted at first hand with books in which are stored the energies of the past, we content ourselves with knowing only something about the men who wrote them. Instead of admiring with our own eyes the architectural beauties of St. Paul's Cathedral, we read a biography of Sir Christopher Wren.

Again, it must be borne in mind that literature is one thing, and the history of literature is another. The study of the latter, however important, cannot be substituted for that of the former; yet it is not desirable to separate the two. To acquire any serviceable knowledge of a book, you will be greatly aided by knowing under what peculiar conditions it was conceived and produced,—the history of the country, the manners of the people, the status of morals and politics at the time it was written. Between history and literature there is a mutual relationship which should not be overlooked. "A book 171is the offspring of the aggregate intellect of humanity," and it gives back to humanity, in the shape of new ideas and new combinations of old ideas, not only all that which it has derived from it, but more,—increased intellectual vitality, and springs of action hitherto unknown.

In the study of literature, one should begin with an author and with a subject not too difficult to understand. A beginner will be likely to find but little comfort in Chaucer or Spenser, or even in Emerson; but after he has worked up to them he may study them with unbounded delight. For a ready understanding and correct appreciation of the great masterpieces of English literature, a knowledge of Greek and Roman mythology and history is almost indispensable. The student will find the courses of historical reading given in a former chapter of this book of much value in supplementing his literary studies.

The great works of the world's masterminds should be studied together, with reference to the similarity of their subject-matter. For example, the reading of Shakspeare will give occasion to the study of dramatic literature in all its forms; the reading of Milton's "Paradise Lost" will introduce us to172the great epics, and to heroic poetry in general; Sir Walter Scott's "Lay of the Last Minstrel" will lead naturally to the romance literature of modern and mediæval times; Chaucer's "Canterbury Tales" fitly illustrate the story-telling phase of poetry; the study of lyric poetry may centre around the old ballads, the poems of Robert Burns, and the religious hymns of our language; Bunyan's "Pilgrim's Progress" introduces us to allegory, and Milton's "Lycidas" to elegiac and pastoral poetry; and to know the best specimens of argumentative prose, we begin with the speeches of Daniel Webster and end with the orations of Demosthenes.

The following schemes for the study of different departments of English literature have been tested both with private students and with classes at school. Of course, many of the books mentioned are to be used chiefly as works of reference; some of them may be conveniently omitted in case it is desirable to abridge the course, and others may be exchanged for similar works upon the same subject.

173

SCHEME I.

For the Study of Dramatic Literature.

LITERATURE.

For manuals use any or all of the following works—

SHAW'S *Manual of English Literature.*

MORLEY'S *First Sketch of English Literature.*

BALDWIN'S *English Literature and Literary Criticism.*

BROOKE'S *Primer of English Literature.*

WELCH'S *Development of English Literature.*

RICHARDSON'S *Familiar Talks on English Literature.*

To be read—

"Rise and Progress of the English Drama," in White's Shakspeare, vol. i.

"Origin and Growth of the Drama in England," in Hudson's *Life, Art, and Characters of Shakspeare*, vol. i.

"Life of Shakspeare" in either of the works just named.

To be referred to—

DOWDEN'S *Shakspere Primer.*

ABBOTT'S *Shakspearian Grammar.*

Taine's English Literature, the chapter on "Shakspeare."

174

To be studied—

I. THE MERCHANT OF VENICE.

II. CORIOLANUS or JULIUS CÆSAR.

III. RICHARD III.

PARALLEL STUDIES.

English histories for study and reference—

GREEN'S *History of the English People.*

KNIGHT'S *History of England.*

YONGE'S *Young Folks' England.*

Study the history of England from 1066 to 1580.

Write an essay on one of the following subjects—

1. Miracles and Mysteries.
2. Popular Amusements of the Middle Ages.
3. The Church and the Early Drama.
4. The Social Condition of England in the Time of Queen Elizabeth.
5. The Early Theatres.

I. Study the history and topography of Venice.

Write essays on various subjects suggested by the play

II. Read Plutarch's Life of Coriolanus or of Julius Cæsar.

Study the peculiarities of Roman life and manners.

Refer to Mommsen's Rome.

III. Study the history of Richard

IV. A Midsummer Night's Dream.

V. King Lear or Macbeth.

VI. Hamlet.

Books for study and reference while studying Shakspeare—

Hazlitt's *Characters of Shakspeare's Plays.*

Coleridge's *Literary Remains.*

Leigh Hunt's *Imagination and Fancy.*

Lamb's *Essay on Shakspeare's Tragedies.*

Dowden's *Mind and Art of Shakspeare.*

Weiss's *Wit, Humor, and Shakspeare.*

Morgan's *The Shakspearian Myth.*

Also, the various works of the Shakspeare Society and of the New Shakspere Society.

III. as related by trustworthy historians. Write an essay in his defence.

IV. Study the sources from which this play has been derived. Write essays on subjects suggested by it.

V. Read Geoffrey of Monmouth's account of King Lear. Learn what you can of the historical legends of early Britain and Scotland.

Write essays on subjects suggested by these plays.

VI. Hamlet. Study the sources of the play. Write essays. Discuss the question of Hamlet's madness.

Write an essay on Shakspeare's works, his life, his art.

Discuss the Baconian theory of the authorship of Shakspeare's plays.

175**General Study of the Drama.**

1. *The Greek Drama.*—Refer to, or read,—

Mahaffy's *Greek Literature.*

Schlegel's *Dramatic Literature.*

Copleston's *Æschylus.*

Church's *Stories from the Greek Tragedians.*

Mrs. Browning's translation of*Prometheus Bound.*

Donne's *Euripides.*

Froude's essay,—*Sea Studies.*

Donaldson's *Theatre of the Greeks.*

2. *The Roman Drama.*—See the following works—

Schlegel's *Dramatic Literature.*

Simcox's *History of Latin Literature.*

Quackenbos's *Classical Literature.*

3. *Mysteries and Miracle-Plays.*—Refer to—

"An Essay on the Origin of the English Stage," in Percy's *Reliques of Ancient English Poetry.*

Warton's *History of English Poetry.*

Morley's *English Writers*; and the

1. *The Greek Drama.*—Study the history of Greece from some brief text-book like Smith's *Smaller History.* Study the life and manners of the Greeks by referring to Becker's *Charicles*, or Mahaffy's *Old Greek Life.*

Refer to Grote and Curtius.

Read the old Greek Myths.

Write essays on the Greek Stage, the Greek Tragedy, and kindred subjects.

Discuss the subjects suggested by reading "Prometheus Bound."

2. Refer to Mommsen's *Rome*, especially the chapters relating to literature and art.

3. Review the history of England from 1066 to 1580, with special reference to the social, religious, and political progress of the people.

essays of White and Hudson, already named.

176

4. *The Elizabethan Drama.*—See the works on Shakspeare, mentioned above; also,—

WHIPPLE'S *Literature of the Age of Elizabeth.*

HAZLITT'S *Age of Elizabeth.*

LAMB'S *Notes on the Elizabethan Dramatists.*

WARD'S *English Dramatic Literature.*

Study selections from—

JONSON'S *Every Man in his Humor.*

MARLOWE'S *Doctor Faustus*, or *Tamburlaine.*

Also, selections from Webster, Beaumont and Fletcher, and others.

5. Study Milton's *Comus.*

Read Milton's *Samson Agonistes.*

6. *The Drama of the Restoration.*—Read—

HAZLITT'S *English Comic Writers.*

JOHNSON'S *Life of Dryden.*

THACKERAY'S *English Humorists.*

MACAULAY'S Essay on the *Comic Dramatists of the Restoration.*

WARD'S *History of the Drama.*

7. *The Later Drama.*—See the following—

FITZGERALD'S *Life of David Garrick.*

The Life and Dramatic Works of R. B. *Sheridan.*

Lives of the Kembles.

MACREADY'S *Reminiscences.*

LEWES'S *Actors and the Art of Acting.*

HUTTON'S *Plays and Players.*

GOLDSMITH'S *She Stoops to Conquer.*

SHERIDAN'S *School for Scandal.*

BULWER'S *Richelieu.*

TENNYSON'S *Drama of Queen Mary.*

SHELLEY'S *Prometheus Unbound.*

SWINBURNE'S *Atalanta in Calydon.*

ROBERT BROWNING'S *Dramas.*

4. Subjects for special study—

The history of the reigns of Elizabeth and James I.

The causes and character of the Renaissance in England.

Character of the Elizabethan dramatists.

Causes of the decline of dramatic literature.

The character of James I.

The Puritans and their influence upon the manners of the English people.

The Puritans and the drama.

PRYNNE'S *Histrio-Mastix.*

The reign of Charles I.

5. Study the history of Oliver Cromwell and Puritan England. Suppression of the drama.

Read Macaulay's *Essay on Milton.*

Write essays on subjects suggested by these studies.

Discuss the character of the Puritans.

6. Study the state of society at the time of the Restoration.

The history of England from 1660 to 1760.

177

Write essays on subjects relating to the drama or the public manners of this period.

JEREMY COLLIER'S work.

7. Study the history of England to the close of the eighteenth century.

Write an essay on the "Influence of the Drama."

Discuss the means by which the stage may be made beneficial as a means of popular education.

Study the character of the drama of our own times, and how it may be improved.

SCHEME II.

For the Study of Epic Poetry.

LITERATURE.

For manuals, etc., see Scheme I.

To be studied—

MILTON'S *Paradise Lost.*

Read—

MACAULAY'S *Essay on Milton.*

DR. JOHNSON'S *Life of Milton.*

STOPFORD BROOKE'S *Milton.*

MARK PATTISON'S *Milton.*

HAZLITT'S Essay on "Shakspeare and Milton," in *English Poets.*

HAZLITT'S Essay on *Milton's Eve.*

DE QUINCEY'S Essay on *Milton vs. Southey and Landor.*

HIMES'S *A Study of Paradise Lost.*

The Spectator; the numbers issued on Saturdays from Jan. 5 to May 3, 1712.

MASSON'S *Introduction to Milton's Poetical Works.*

GOSSE'S Essay on Milton and Vondel, in "Studies in Northern Literature."

Refer to—

MASSON'S *Life of Milton.*

BOYD'S *Milton's Paradise Lost* (with copious notes).

178

A notice of the other great Epics—

1. HOMER'S *Iliad and Odyssey.* Selections read and studied.

(See list of books suggested for the study of Greek history, etc.)

2. VIRGIL'S *Æneid* (Morris's translation). General plan of the work observed.

3. DANTE'S *Divina Commedia*(Longfellow's or Carey's translation). General plan of the work observed.

179

Attempted Epics—

COWLEY'S *Davideis.*

GLOVER'S *Leonidas.*

SOUTHEY'S *Joan of Arc*, *Madoc*,*Thalaba*, and *The Curse of Kehama.*

LANDOR'S *Gebir.*

Why these poems fail to be epics.

PARALLEL STUDIES.

For English histories, see Scheme I.

Read the account of the Creation as related in the book of Genesis.

Study the character of the Puritans in England.

Write essays on subjects suggested by the study of "Paradise Lost."

Study the mythological allusions found in the poem. The following works of reference are recommended for this purpose—

SMITH'S *Classical Dictionary.*

MURRAY'S *Manual of Mythology.*

KEIGHTLEY'S *Classical Mythology.*

Write an essay on the general plan of the poem.

Discuss Milton's theory of the universe as understood from the reading of "Paradise Lost."

See list of books elsewhere given, relating to Greek Mythology, the Trojan War, etc.

See—

LOWELL'S Essay on Dante, in *Among My Books.*

SYMOND'S *Introduction to the Study of Dante.*

BOTTA'S *Dante as a Philosopher, Patriot, and Poet.*

CARLYLE'S *Heroes and Hero-Worship.*

Historical studies suggested by these attempted poems.

Write an essay on the qualities requisite to a great epic poem.

Discuss the possibility of another great epic being written.

Heroic Poems—

BARBOUR'S Bruce.

DAVENANT'S Gondibert.

The Mock-Heroic—

POPE'S *Rape of the Lock*. The general plan. Selections studied.

Study the legends and historical events upon which these poems are founded.

Write an essay on some subject suggested by these studies.

SCHEME III.

For the Study of Poetical Romance.

LITERATURE.

For manuals, see Scheme I.

To be studied— Sir Walter Scott's great poems,—

The Lay of the Last Minstrel.

Marmion.

The Lady of the Lake.

To be read—

CARLYLE'S Essay on *Sir Walter Scott.*

HAZLITT on Scott, in *The Spirit of the Age.*

The chapter on Scott in Shaw's*Manual of English Literature.*

180

R. H. HUTTON'S *Sir Walter Scott*, in "English Men of Letters."

How the Romance poetry differed from Classic poetry.

See Macaulay's Essay on *Southey's Life of Byron.*

The Origin of Romance Literature.— Refer to—

WARTON'S *History of Poetry.*

The Introduction to Ellis's *Early English Metrical Romances.*

RITSON'S *Ancient English Metrical Romances.*

PERCY'S *Reliques*, introductory essay to book iii.

To be studied—

TENNYSON'S *Idylls of the King.*

Refer to Taine's criticism of Tennyson's Poetry, in his *English Literature*, vol. iv.

Read selected portions of Byron's poetical romances—

PARALLEL STUDIES.

For histories, see Scheme I.

Read the history of Scotland from the earliest period to the reign of James V.

MISS PORTER'S *Scottish Chiefs.*

SCOTT'S *Minstrelsy of the Scottish Border.*

AYTOUN'S *Ballads of Scotland.*

SCOTT'S *Fair Maid of Perth.*

Write essays on subjects suggested by these studies.

Discuss the character of the Scotch people in feudal times.

Compare selections from Scott with selections from Pope. Find other illustrations of the difference between the two schools of poetry.

Read the chapter on the Troubadours, in Sismondi's *Literature of Southern Europe*; also in Van Laun's *History of French Literature.*

Refer to Miss Prescott's*Troubadours and Trouvères.*

Read the account of the romances of King Arthur as related in the books already mentioned.

Also,—

LANIER'S *Boy's King Arthur.*

BULFINCH'S *Age of Chivalry.*

GEOFFREY OF MONMOUTH'S *British History*, books viii. and ix.

Write an essay on the King Arthur legends.

Compare Byron's poetry with that of Sir Walter Scott,

The Giaour.
The Corsair.
The Bride of Abydos.
The Siege of Corinth.

Read *Byron*, by John Nichol, in "English Men of Letters."

Read Matthew Arnold's Introduction to the *Selected Poems of Lord Byron.*

1st. As to matter.
2d. As to style.

Write essays on subjects suggested by these studies.

Discuss reasons why Lord Byron's poetry is much less popular than formerly.

181

Study selections from Moore's *Lalla Rookh.*

Read Hazlitt's criticisms on Moore, in his "English Poets."

Also, W. M. Rossetti's Introduction to the *Poems of Thomas Moore.*

Study, from whatever sources are available, Oriental life and manners as portrayed in *Lalla Rookh.* Write essays on the same.

Study selections from Morris's*Sigurd the Volsung*; also from *The Earthly Paradise* by the same author.

Study the myths of the north, referring to Mallet's *Northern Antiquities* and Anderson's *Norse Mythology.*

SCHEME IV.

For the Study of Story-Telling Poetry.

LITERATURE.

Use manuals for reference as indicated in Scheme I. To these may be added Underwood's *American Literature*, and White's *Story of English Literature.*

CHAUCER'S *Canterbury Tales.*

Study the *Prologue* and either the*Knightes Tale* or the *Clerkes Tale.*

Refer to, or read,—

The Riches of Chaucer, by Charles Cowden Clarke.

LOWELL'S Essay on *Chaucer*, in "My Study Windows."

CARPENTER'S *English of the Fourteenth Century.*

Chaucer's Canterbury Tales Explained, by Saunders.

Canterbury Chimes, by Storr and Turner.

Stories from Old English Poetry, by Mrs. Richardson.

PARALLEL STUDIES.

Use for reference, Green's *History of the English People*, or Knight's *History of England*; also, some standard history of America.

Study the history of England in the fourteenth century, and especially the social condition of the people during that period.

Make some acquaintance with the great Italian writers who flourished about this time, and exerted a marked influence upon Chaucer's work.

Refer to—

SISMONDI'S *Literature of Southern Europe*;

CAMPBELL'S *Life of Petrarch*;

BOTTA'S *Dante as Philosopher, Patriot, and Poet*; etc.

182

Read some of Scott's shorter narrative poems,—

Rokeby.
The Bridal of Triermain.
Harold the Dauntless.

For criticisms and essays on Scott, see Scheme III.

Study the historical subjects, suggested by these poems.

See Parallel Studies in connection with Scott's longer poems, Scheme III.

Study *The Prisoner of Chillon*, by

See criticisms on Byron, in

Lord Byron.

Read Wordsworth's story-poems,—

The White Doe of Rylstone;

Peter Bell;

We are Seven; etc.

Study Coleridge's *The Ancient Mariner*, and Keats's *The Eve of St. Agnes*.

For criticisms on the poets last read, refer to—

HAZLITT'S *English Poets*.

SWINBURNE'S *Studies and Essays*.

SHAIRP'S *Studies in Poetry*.

LORD HOUGHTON'S *Life of Keats*.

MATTHEW ARNOLD'S Essay on Keats, in Ward's *English Poets*.

CARLYLE'S *Reminiscences*.

Read Campbell's *Gertrude of Wyoming*.

Read selections from Mrs. Hemans.

Read Mrs. Browning's *Lady Geraldine's Courtship*; also some of her shorter poems.

Study Tennyson's poems,—

The Princess.

Maud.

Enoch Arden.

Also his shorter poems.

183

Study at least two poems in Morris's*Earthly Paradise*.

Study Longfellow's poems,—

Evangeline.

Miles Standish.

Hiawatha.

Tales of a Wayside Inn.

The Skeleton in Armor.

Read Underwood's *Life of Longfellow*.

Study the story-poems of John G. Whittier: *Maud Muller*, *Flud Ireson*; etc.

Taine's*English Literature*.

Read Hazlitt's estimate of Wordsworth, in *The Spirit of the Age*.

DE QUINCEY on Wordsworth's poetry, in *Literary Criticism*.

Write essays on subjects suggested by these studies.

Study the history of the English people from 1760 to 1820, with special reference to their social condition, and the progress of literature.

Write essays on suggested subjects.

Read the historical account of the Massacre of Wyoming.

Read biographies of Mrs. Hemans and Mrs. Browning. Discuss reasons why Mrs. Hemans' poetry is no longer popular.

Consult—

STEDMAN'S *Victorian Poets*.

HADLEY'S *Essays*.

KINGSLEY'S *Miscellanies*.

Study the classical and Norse legends upon which these stories are based.

See—

BANCROFT'S *History of the United States*, vol. iv.

ABBOTT'S *Life of Miles Standish*.

Study other historical references, etc., suggested by these poems.

Write essays on subjects suggested by these studies.

SCHEME V.

For the Study of Allegory.

LITERATURE.

ÆSOP'S Fables.

Oriental parables and fables.

Study Bunyan's *Pilgrim's Progress*, as being the most popular allegory in the English language.

Read—

PARALLEL STUDIES.

Rhetorical definition of allegory. The distinction between fables and parables.

Study the history of the rise and progress of Puritanism in England.

Refer to Green's *History of the*

MACAULAY'S *Essay on John Bunyan.*
CHEEVER'S *Lectures on Bunyan.*
184
Anglo-Saxon parables and allegories. The growth of the allegory.
The Vision of Piers Plowman.
The great French allegory, the *Roman de la Rose.*
CHAUCER'S *Romaunt of the Rose.*
Other allegorical poems usually ascribed to Chaucer,—
The Court of Love.
The Cuckow and the Nightingale.
The Parlament of Foules.
The Flower and the Leaf.
Refer to Taine's *English Literature.*
Notice, next, Dunbar's *The Thistle and the Rose*; also, *The Golden Terge*, and the *Dance of the Seven Sins.*
STEPHEN HAWES'S *Grand Amour and la Bell Pucell.*
Study selected passages from Spenser's *Faerie Queene*; also the general plan of the poem.
See—
LOWELL'S *Among My Books.*
CRAIK'S *Spenser and his Poetry.*
Read—
PHINEAS FLETCHER'S *Purple Island.*
THOMSON'S *Castle of Indolence.*
LOWELL'S *Vision of Sir Launfal.*
GAY'S *Fables.*
BURNS'S *The Twa Dogs*, and *The Brigs of Ayr.*
Abou Ben Adhem.
185

English People, and to Taine's *English Literature.*
Consult—
MORLEY'S *English Writers.*
WARTON'S *History of English Poetry.*
GEORGE P. MARSH'S *Lectures on the Origin and History of the English Language.*
SKEATS'S *Specimens of English Literature.*
Study the social condition of England in the thirteenth, fourteenth, and fifteenth centuries. Refer to the histories already mentioned; also to—
PEARSON'S *History of England in the Fourteenth Century.*
LANIER'S *Boy's Froissart*, or the abridged edition of *Froissart's Chronicles.*
TOWLE'S *History of Henry V.*
Study the social and literary history of England during the sixteenth century.
Refer to Froude's *History of England.*
Write essays on subjects suggested by these studies.

Discuss the value of allegory as an aid in education.
Why has the taste for allegory steadily declined?
Write in plain prose the lesson learned in each of the fables studied.
What relationship exists between fables and myths?

SCHEME VI.
For the Study of Didactic Poetry.

LITERATURE.

DRYDEN'S *Religio Laici*; and *The Hind and the Panther.*
Study selected passages from Pope's*Essay on Criticism*, and *Essay on Man.*
YOUNG'S *Night Thoughts.*
JOHNSON'S *Vanity of Human Wishes.*
AKENSIDE'S *Pleasures of the Imagination.*
WARTON'S *Pleasures of Melancholy.*
ROGERS' *Pleasures of Memory.*
CAMPBELL'S *Pleasures of Hope.*
GRAHAME'S *The Sabbath.*

REFERENCES.

Refer to—
HAZLITT'S *English Poets*; Lowell's*Among My Books* (essay on Dryden); Macaulay's Essay on Dryden; and Taine's *English Literature.*
JOHNSON'S *Lives of the Poets*; Stephen's*Hours in a Library*; De Quincey's*Literature of the Eighteenth Century.*
MACAULAY'S Essay on *Samuel Johnson*; Boswell's *Life of Dr. Johnson*; Carlyle's Essay on*Boswell's Life of Johnson*; Stephen's *Johnson*, in "English Men of Letters."

Study selected passages from Wordsworth's *Excursion*.

Select and study some of the best-known shorter didactic poems in the language.

186

WHIPPLE'S Essay on Wordsworth, in "Literature and Life."

SHAIRP'S *Studies in Poetry and Philosophy*; Hazlitt's *Spirit of the Age*; Charles Lamb's Essay on Wordsworth's *Excursion.*

SCHEME VII.

For the Study of Lyric Poetry.

LITERATURE. | PARALLEL STUDIES.

I.

The Early Ballads.

Ballads of Robin Hood.

Ballads of the Scottish Border.

Modern Ballads.

Read histories and stories of the mediæval times.

Refer to Percy's *Reliques*; Aytoun's*Scottish Ballads*; Scott's *Minstrelsy of the Scottish Border.*

II.

Songs of Patriotism.

Read and study the best-known patriotic poems in the language.

Study the historical events, or other circumstances which led to the production of these poems.

III.

Battle Songs.

The battle scenes in Scott's poems. Burns: "Scots wha hae wi' Wallace bled." Macaulay's *Battle of Ivry, Naseby, Horatius at the Bridge.* Tennyson's *Charge of the Light Brigade.* Drayton's *Battle of Agincourt.*

Study the historical events which gave rise to these poems.

Write essays on subjects suggested by these studies.

IV.

Religions Songs and Hymns.

GEORGE HERBERT'S *Temple.* Read selections from Crashaw and Vaughan. Study Milton's *Hymn on the Nativity*, and selections from Keble's *Christian Year.* Read Pope's *Universal Prayer*, and *The Dying Christian*; also selections from Moore's *Sacred Songs*, Byron's *Hebrew Melodies*, and Milman's *Hymns for Church Service.*

For specimens and extracts of lyric poetry of every class, consult Ward's*English Poets*; Appleton's *Library of British Poets*; *The Family Library of British Poets*; Emerson's *Parnassus*; Chambers' *Cyclopædia of English Literature*; Bryant's *Library of Poetry and Song*; and Piatt's *American Poetry and Art.*

187V.

Love Lyrics.

The Songs of the Troubadours. Wyatt's Poems. Marlowe's *Passionate Shepherd*. Raleigh's *The Nymph's Reply*. Robert Herrick's Poems. Selections from the poems of Sir John Suckling. The love poems of Robert Burns. Coleridge's*Genevieve*. Selections from other poets.

Consult Miss Prescott's*Troubadours and Trouvères*; Warton's*History of English Poetry*. Study the biographies of Marlowe, Raleigh, Herrick, and Suckling. Read Carlyle's Essay on *Robert Burns*; and Principal Shairp's *Burns*, in "English Men of Letters."

VI.

Sonnets.

The origin of the sonnet. Selections from the sonnets of Wyatt, Spenser, Sidney, Shakspeare, Drayton, Drummond, Milton, Wordsworth, Keats, and others. Mrs. Browning's *Sonnets from the Portuguese*.

See Leigh Hunt's *Book of the Sonnet*; Dennis's *English Sonnets*; French's *Dublin Afternoon Lectures*; Massey's *Shakspeare's Sonnets*; Henry Brown's *Sonnets of Shakspeare Solved*; Tomlinson's *The Sonnet: its Origin, Structure, and Place in Poetry*.

VII.

Odes.

DRYDEN'S *Alexander's Feast*.

POPE'S *Ode on St. Cecilia's Day*.

COLLINS'S *Ode on the Passions*, and other odes.

GRAY'S *Ode on the Progress of Poesy*, and *The Bard*.

KEATS'S *Sleep and Poetry*.

SHELLEY'S *Ode to Liberty*, and *To the West Wind*.

COLERIDGE'S *Ode on France*, and *To the Departing Year*.

WORDSWORTH'S *Ode on the Intimations of Immortality*.

See Husk's Account of the Musical Celebrations on St. Cecilia's Day, in the Sixteenth, Seventeenth, and Eighteenth Centuries.

Study the construction of the ode. Compare the English ode with the Greek and Latin ode. Learn something of the odes of Horace.

Write essays on subjects suggested by these studies.

188VIII.

Elegies.

Study Milton's *Lycidas*. Read selections from Spenser's *Astrophel*; Shelley's *Adonais*; Tennyson's *In Memoriam*; *Ode on the Death of the Duke of Wellington*; Pope's *Elegy on an Unfortunate Lady*. Study Gray's*Elegy in a Country Churchyard*; The Dirge in *Cymbeline*; and Collins's*Dirge in Cymbeline*. Read Shenstone's*Elegies*; Cowper's *The Castaway*;

For references to Milton and Spenser, see other schemes. For Shelley's *Adonais*, see Hutton's*Essays*. See F. W. Robertson's *Analysis of In Memoriam*. See also, for subjects connected with these studies, Roscoe's*Essays*; Hazlitt's *English Poets*; Dr. Johnson's *Life of Gray*; E. W. Gosse's*Gray*, in "English Men of Letters;" Parke Godwin's *Life of William* and Bryant's *Thanatopsis*.

Cullen Bryant.

IX.

Miscellaneous Lyrics.

Study selections from the poems of Burns, Ramsay, and Fergusson; Whittier, Bryant, and Longfellow; William Blake; Mrs. Browning, Tennyson, and Swinburne; and others, both British and American.

Refer to the manuals elsewhere mentioned.

Write essays on subjects suggested by these studies.

Discuss the distinctive qualities of Lyric Poetry, and the place which it occupies in English Literature.

189

SCHEME VIII.

For the Study of Descriptive Poetry, Etc.

LITERATURE.

Study selections from the poems of William Cullen Bryant.

Study Whittier's *Snow-Bound*, and other descriptive poems.

Study Milton's *L'Allegro* and *Il Penseroso*.

Study selections from Thomson's*Seasons*, and Cowper's *Task*.

Study Goldsmith's *Traveller*, and*The Deserted Village*; also, Shenstone's *Schoolmistress*.

Find and read characteristic descriptive passages in the poems of Scott, Byron, Shelley, Wordsworth, Keats, Browning, and others. Compare Scott's descriptions with the descriptions in Pope's *Windsor Forest*and in Denham's *Cooper's Hill*.

Select and study descriptive passages from Chaucer's Poems, and from Spenser's *Faerie Queene*.

Read selections from Gay's *Rural Sports*, and from Bloomfield's*Farmer's Boy*.

PARALLEL STUDIES.

See Godwin's *Life of William Cullen Bryant*; and Underwood's biography of John G. Whittier. See Stopford Brooke's *Milton*; and Mark Pattison's*Milton*, in "English Men of Letters;" Irving's *Life of Goldsmith*; Thackeray's*English Humorists of the Eighteenth Century*; William Black's *Goldsmith*, in "English Men of Letters;" Hazlitt's*English Poets*; and De Quincey's*Literature of the Eighteenth Century*.

Read Macaulay's Essay on *Moore's Life of Byron*.

Refer to Goldwin Smith's *Cowper*, in "English Men of Letters;" also to Charles Cowden Clarke's *Life of Cowper*.

See references to Chaucer and Spenser elsewhere given.

Pastoral Poetry.

Study Milton's *Arcades*, and selections from Pope's *Pastorals*; also from Spenser's *Shepherd's Calendar*.

See Drayton's *Shepherd's Garland*; Browne's *Britannia's Pastorals*; Jonson's *Sad Shepherd*; Fletcher's*Faithful Shepherdess*; Gay's*Shepherd's Week*; Ramsay's *Gentle Shepherd*; and Shenstone's *Pastoral Ballads*.

190

Read Pope's *Essay on Pastoral Poetry*.

Learn something about Theocritus and his *Idyls*, and about the *Eclogues*of Virgil. A translation of the former may be found in Bohn's Classical Library. The latest translation of the*Eclogues* is that by Wilstach.

SCHEME IX.

For the Study of Satire, Wit, and Humor.

LITERATURE.

DEAN SWIFT, the great English satirist. Study his life and character. See Forster's *Life of Swift*; or Leslie Stephen's *Swift*, in "English Men of Letters."

Read selections from *Gulliver's Travels*, and the *Tale of a Tub*. Read, also, his *Modest Proposal.*

DANIEL DEFOE'S Satirical Essays: *The Shortest Way with Dissenters*, etc.

See Minto's *Defoe*, in "English Men of Letters."

The origin and growth of satirical literature in England.

JOHN SKELTON'S *Satires.* See Warton's *History of English Poetry*, and Taine's *English Literature.*

BARCLAY'S *Shyp of Fooles.* See Warton's History.

The Satires of Surrey and Wyatt. See Hallam's *Literary History*, and Chalmers' *Collection of the Poets.*

GASCOIGNE'S *The Steele Glass.*

DONNE'S *Satires.* See Pope's *The Satires of Dr. Donne Versified.*

HALL'S *Virgidemiarum.* See Warton's*History*, and Campbell's*Specimens of the English Poets.*

Study selected passages from Butler's *Hudibras.*

Refer to Hazlitt's *Comic Writers*, and Leigh Hunt's *Wit and Wisdom.*

DRYDEN'S *Absalom and Achitophel*, and the publications which followed it.

191

DRYDEN'S *MacFlecknoe.*

POPE'S *Dunciad.*

BYRON'S *English Bards and Scotch Reviewers.*

LOWELL'S *Fable for Critics.*

POPE'S *Moral Essays.*

SWIFT'S Satirical Poems.

The humor of Fielding, Smollett, and Goldsmith, as exhibited in their writings.

CHATTERTON'S *Prophecy.*

Read Burns' *Holy Willie's Prayer*, and the *Holy Fair.*

SYDNEY SMITH. See the *Wit and Wisdom of Sydney Smith* (1861).

PARALLEL STUDIES.

RABELAIS, the great satirist of France. Read Besant's *French Humorists*; and *Rabelais*, by the same author. Refer also to Van Laun's *History of French Literature.*

VOLTAIRE, the third of the great modern satirists. Read Parton's *Life of Voltaire*; or *Voltaire*, by John Morley; or Colonel Hamley's *Voltaire*, in "Foreign Classics for English Readers."

Satirical literature in Rome.

The great poetical satirists of ancient times,—Horace and Juvenal. See Lord Lytton's translation of the*Epodes and Satires of Horace*; and Dryden's *Imitations of Juvenal.* Dr. Johnson's *London*and *The Vanity of Human Wishes*are also imitations of Juvenal. See Dryden's *Essay on Satire.*

To understand the satires of Hall, Butler, Dryden, and Pope, it is absolutely necessary to be well acquainted with the history and social condition of England during the seventeenth century.

Study Green's *History of the English People.*

Study the political agitations in England just preceding the Revolution of 1688.

Compare these four personal satires, and write essays on the subjects suggested by their study.

Read Thackeray's *Humorists of the Eighteenth Century*, and Hazlitt's*Comic Writers.*

Study the social condition of England in the eighteenth century.

Study the political agitations in England during the first half of the

The Fudge Family in Paris, by Thomas Moore.

The Humorous Essays of Charles Lamb.

THOMAS CARLYLE'S *Sartor Resartus*, and *Latter-Day Pamphlets*. Study selections.

192

THACKERAY as a humorist. Read his *Irish Sketch-Book*, and selections from the *Book of Snobs*, but especially observe his power in *Vanity Fair*.

Read and study Dr. Holmes' *Autocrat of the Breakfast-Table*.

Read Lowell's *Biglow Papers*.

Read selections from Mark Twain and other living American humorists.

Compare the humor of the present day with that of the last generation. Read selections from Irving's *Sketch Book*, and *Knickerbocker's New York*.

Read Burns' *Tam O'Shanter*; and selections from Hood, John G. Saxe, and others.

present century. Refer to *Knight's History of England*, and to Justin McCarthy's *History of Our Own Times*. Miss Martineau's *History of the Thirty Years' Peace* may be read with profit.

Write essays on subjects suggested by these studies.

Study the true distinctions between Wit, Humor, and Satire; and select from what you have read a number of illustrative examples.

Discuss questions which may arise from these studies; and write essays on the same.

Study the biographies of Irving, Lowell, Holmes, Mark Twain, Saxe, and other American authors whose works have been noticed in this scheme.

SCHEME X.

For the Study of English Prose Fiction.

General Works of Reference.

LITERATURE.

DUNLOP'S *History of Fiction*.

JEAFFRESON'S *Novels and Novelists*.

MASSON'S *British Novelists and their Styles*.

TUCKERMAN'S *History of English Prose Fiction*.

PARALLEL STUDIES.

The historical works and also the literary manuals mentioned in Scheme IV. should be at hand for constant reference.

1931.

The First Romances.

SIDNEY'S *Arcadia*.

LYLY'S *Euphues*.

GREENE'S *Pandosto, or the Triumph of Time*.

The Novels of Thomas Nash.

Study the conditions of life and thought in England under which these first attempts at the writing of prose romance were made.

II.

Fabulous Voyages and Travels.

GODWIN'S *Man in the Moon*.

HALL'S *Mundus Alter et Idem*.

SWIFT'S *Gulliver's Travels*;—read

See Collins' *Lucian*, in "Ancient Classics for English Readers," for an account of Lucian's *Veracious History*.

selections.

Study *Robinson Crusoe.*

The Adventures of Peter Wilkins.

EDGAR A. POE'S *Narrative of Arthur Gordon Pym.*

Read the voyage of Gargantua by Rabelais; or, better, consult Besant's*Rabelais.*

Read Minto's *Defoe*, in "English Men of Letters."

See Forster's *Life of Dean Swift*; Scott's *Memoir of Dean Swift*; and Minto's *Manual of English Prose.*

III.

Romances of the Supernatural.

WALPOLE'S *The Castle of Otranto.*

MRS. RADCLIFFE'S *Romances.*

GODWIN'S *St. Leon.*

BULWER'S *Zanoni.*

MRS. SHELLEY'S *Frankenstein.*

LEWIS'S *The Monk.*

See Tuckerman's *Literature of Fiction* (an essay); C. Kegan Paul's*Life of William Godwin*; Macaulay's Essay on *Horace Walpole*; Miss Kavanagh's *English Women of Letters.*

IV.

Oriental Romances

BECKFORD'S *Vathek.*

HOPE'S *Anastasius.*

The Adventures of Hajji Baba.

194V.

Historical Romances.

MISS PORTER'S *Scottish Chiefs.*

SCOTT'S *Waverley Novels.*

The Novels of G. P. R. James.

BULWER'S *Last Days of Pompeii*;*Rienzi*; *Harold*; *The Last of the Barons.*

LOCKHART'S *Valerius.*

KINGSLEY'S *Hypatia.*

GEORGE ELIOT'S *Romola.*

See Lockhart's *Life of Scott*; Stephen's *Hours in a Library*; Carlyle's Essay on *Sir Walter Scott*; Shaw's *Manual of English Literature*; Hutton's *Scott*, in "English Men of Letters;" Nassau Senior's *Essays on Fiction*; *The Life of Edward Bulwer-Lytton*, by his son, the present Lord Lytton.

VI.

Novels of Social Life, etc.

RICHARDSON'S *Novels.*

FIELDING'S *Tom Jones.*

SMOLLETT'S Novels.

STERNE'S *Tristram Shandy.*

GOLDSMITH'S *Vicar of Wakefield.*

MISS BURNEY'S Novels.

GODWIN'S *Caleb Williams.*

MISS EDGEWORTH'S Novels.

SCOTT'S *Guy Mannering*;

See Stephen's *Hours in a Library*; Hazlitt's *English Novelists*; Thackeray's *English Humorists of the Eighteenth Century*; Irving's *Life of Goldsmith*; Macaulay's Essay on*Madame d'Arblay*; Miss Kavanagh's*English Women of Letters*; James T. Fields' *Yesterdays with Authors*; Horne's *New Spirit of the Age*; John Forster's *Life of Charles Dickens*;

The Heart of Mid-Lothian;
The Bride of Lammermoor;
The Antiquary; etc.
MISS AUSTEN'S Works.
THACKERAY'S *Vanity Fair.*
DICKENS'S *Pickwick Papers.*
Other Novels of Dickens and Thackeray.
CHARLOTTE BRONTË'S *Jane Eyre.*
BULWER'S Novels.
DISRAELI'S *Vivian*; and *Lothair.*
CHARLES KINGSLEY'S Novels.
GEORGE ELIOT'S Works.

Hannay's *Studies on Thackeray*; Hannay's *Characters and Sketches*; Anthony Trollope's *Thackeray*, in "English Men of Letters;" Taine's*English Literature*, vol. iv.; Mrs. Gaskell's *Life of Charlotte Brontë*; Miss Martineau's *Biographical Sketches*; Thackeray's *Roundabout Papers*; Life of *Charles Brockden Brown*, in Sparks' "American Biography;" Griswold's *Prose*

195

American Fiction—
CHARLES BROCKDEN BROWN'S *Wieland*, and other Novels.
COOPER'S Novels.
JAMES KIRKE PAULDING.
JOHN P. KENNEDY.
WILLIAM GILMORE SIMMS.
HAWTHORNE'S Works.
The later and living novelists.

Writers of America; Prescott's*Miscellaneous Essays*; J. T. Fields'*Hawthorne*; H. A. Page's *Life of Hawthorne*; Lathrop's *Study of Hawthorne*; Roscoe's *Essays*;*Hawthorne*, by Henry James, in "English Men of Letters;" Cooke's*George Eliot: a Critical Study of her Life, Writings, and Philosophy*; (Round-Table Series) *George Eliot, Moralist and Thinker.*

VII.

Didactic Fiction.

MORE'S *Utopia.*
HARRINGTON'S *Oceana.*
DISRAELI'S *Coningsby.*
BULWER-LYTTON'S *The Coming Race.*
BUNYAN'S *Pilgrim's Progress.*
HANNAH MORE'S Novels.
JOHNSON'S *Rasselas.*
The modern didactic novel.

See Hallam's *Literary History*; and references given in the preceding schemes.

196

An After Word.

HERE let us face the last question of all: In the shade and valley of Life, on what shall we repose? When we must withdraw from the scenes which our own energies and agonies have somewhat helped to make glorious; when the windows are darkened, and the sound of the grinding is low,—where shall we find the beds of asphodel? Can any couch be more delectable than that amidst the Elysian leaves of Books? The occupations of the morning and the noon determine the affections, which will continue to seek their old nourishment when the grand climacteric has been reached.

THE AUTHOR OF "HESPERIDES."

197-9

INDEX.

FOOTNOTES:

1 Robert Collyer: *Addresses and Sermons.*

2 *The Doctor*, Interchapter V., 1856.

3 Arthur Schopenhauer: *Parerga und Paralipomena*, 1851.

4 *The Elements of Drawing, in Three Letters to Beginners*, 1857.

5 *The Spectator*, No. 166.

6 *Fortnightly Review* (April, 1879),—"On the Choice of Books."

7 *Parerga und Paralipomena* (1851).

8 *The Critic* (July 5, 1884),—"Leisure Reading."

9 John Ruskin: *Sesame and Lilies.*

10 *Guesses at Truth, by Two Brothers*, 1848.

11 *Society and Solitude*,—"Books."

12 George Gilfillan.

13 *Friends in Council.*

14 *Views and Opinions*, by Matthew Browne (W. H. Rands).

15 *The Choice of Books.*

16 *Temple Bar* (September, 1884),—"Barry Cornwall on the Reading of Books."

17 *Sesame and Lilies.*

18 *Meliora* (October, 1867).

19 Sparks's *Life of Franklin*, part i.

20 *My Schools and Schoolmasters.*

21 *Memoir of Robert Chambers: with Autobiographic Reminiscences of William Chambers.*

22 *Chinese Classics*, by J. Legge. 3 vols.

23 Frederic Harrison: *Fortnightly Review* (April, 1879), "On the Choice of Books."

BIOGRAPHIES OF MUSICIANS.

LIFE OF LISZT. With Portrait.
LIFE OF HAYDN. With Portrait.
LIFE OF MOZART. With Portrait.
LIFE OF WAGNER. With Portrait.
LIFE OF BEETHOVEN. With Portrait.

From the German of Dr. Louis Nohl.

In cloth, per volume	$ 1.25
The same, in neat box, per set	6.25
In half calf, per set	13.75

Of the "Life of Liszt," the *Herald* (Boston) says: "It is written in great simplicity and perfect taste, and is wholly successful in all that it undertakes to portray."

Of the "Life of Haydn," the *Gazette* (Boston) says: "No fuller history of Haydn's career, the society in which he moved, and of his personal life can be found than is given in this work."

Of the "Life of Mozart," the *Standard* says: "Mozart supplies a fascinating subject for biographical treatment. He lives in these pages somewhat as the world saw him, from his marvellous boyhood till his untimely death."

Of the "Life of Wagner," the *American* (Baltimore) says: "It gives in vigorous outlines those events of the life of the tone poet which exercised the greatest influences upon his artistic career.... It is a story of a strange life devoted to lofty aims."

Of the "Life of Beethoven," the *National Journal of Education* says: "Beethoven was great and noble as a man, and his artistic creations were in harmony with his great nature. The story of his life, outlined in this volume, is of the deepest interest."

TALES FROM FOREIGN TONGUES.

MEMORIES. A Story of German Love. By MAX MULLER.
GRAZIELLA. A Story of Italian Love. By A. DE LAMARTINE.
MADELEINE. A Story of French Love. By JULES SANDEAU.
MARIE. A Story of Russian Love. By ALEX. PUSHKIN.

In cloth, full gilt, per volume	$1.25
The same, in neat box, per set	5.00
In half calf or morocco, per set	12.00

The series of four volumes forms, perhaps, the choicest addition to the English language that has been made in recent years.

Of "Memories," the London *Academy* says: "It is a prose poem.... Its beauty and pathos show us a fresh phase of a many-sided mind, to which we already owe large debts of gratitude."

Of "Graziella," the Boston *Post* says: "It is full of beautiful sentiment, unique and graceful in style, of course, as were all the writings that left the hands of this distinguished French author."

Of "Madeleine," the New York *Evening Mail* says: "It is one of the most exquisite love tales that ever was written, abounding in genuine pathos and sparkling wit, and so pure in its sentiment that it may be read by a child."

Of "Marie," the Cincinnati *Gazette* says: "It is one of the purest, sweetest little narratives that we have read for a long time. It is a little classic, and a Russian classic, too."

FAMILIAR TALKS ON ENGLISH LITERATURE. A Manual embracing the Great Epochs of English Literature, from the English conquest of Britain, 449, to the death of Walter Scott, 1832. By ABBY SAGE RICHARDSON. Fourth edition, revised. Price $1.75.

The Boston Transcript says:

"The work shows thorough study and excellent judgment, and we can warmly recommend it to schools and private classes for reading as an admirable text-book."

The New York Evening Mail says:

"What the author proposed to do was to convey to her readers a clear idea of the variety, extent, and richness of English literature.... She has done just what she intended to do, and done it well."

The New York Nation says:

"It is refreshing to find a book designed for young readers which seeks to give only what will accomplish the real aim of the study; namely, to excite an interest in English literature, cultivate a taste for what is best in it, and thus lay a foundation on which they can build after reading."

Prof. Moses Coit Tyler says:

"I have had real satisfaction in looking over the book. There are some opinions with which I do not agree; but the main thing about the book is a good thing; namely, its hearty, wholesome love of English literature, and the honest, unpretending, but genial and conversational, manner in which that love is uttered. It is a charming book to read, and it will breed in its readers the appetite to read English literature for themselves."

TALES OF ANCIENT GREECE. By the Rev. Sir G. W. COX, Bart., M.A., Trinity College, Oxford.

12mo, extra, cloth, black and gilt, $1.50.

"Written apparently for young readers, it yet possesses a charm of manner which will recommend it to all."—*The Examiner, London.*

"It is only when we take up such a book as this that we realize how rich in interest is the mythology of Greece."—*Inquirer, Philadelphia.*

"Admirable in style, and level with a child's comprehension. These versions might well find a place in every family."—*The Nation, New York.*

"The author invests these stories with a charm of narrative entirely peculiar. The book is a rich one in every way."—*Standard, Chicago.*

"In Mr. Cox will be found yet another name to be enrolled among those English writers who have vindicated for this country an honorable rank in the investigation of Greek history."—*Edinburgh Review.*

"It is doubtful if these tales—antedating history in their origin, and yet fresh with all the charms of youth to all who read them for the first time—were ever before presented in so chaste and popular form."—*Golden Rule, Boston.*

"The grace with which these old tales of the mythology are re-told makes them as enchanting to the young as familiar fairy tales or the 'Arabian Nights.'... We do not know of a Christmas book which promises more lasting pleasures."—*Publishers' Weekly.*

"Its exterior fits it to adorn the drawing-room table, while its contents are adapted to the entertainment of the most cultivated intelligence.... The book is a scholarly production, and a welcome addition to a department of literature that is thus far quite too scantily furnished."—*Tribune, Chicago.*

SHORT HISTORY OF FRANCE, FOR YOUNG PEOPLE. By Miss E. S. KIRKLAND, author of "Six Little Cooks," "Dora's Housekeeping," &c.

12mo, extra, cloth, black and gilt, $1.50.

"A very ably written sketch of French history, from the earliest times to the foundation of the existing Republic."—*Cincinnati Gazette.*

"The narrative is not dry on a single page, and the little history may be commended as the best of its kind that has yet appeared."—*Bulletin, Philadelphia.*

"A book both instructive and entertaining. It is not a dry compendium of dates and facts, but a charmingly written history."—*Christian Union, New York.*

"After a careful examination of its contents, we are able to conscientiously give it our heartiest commendation. We know no elementary history of France that can at all be compared with it."—*Living Church.*

"A spirited and entertaining sketch of the French people and nation,—one that will seize and hold the attention of all bright boys and girls who have a chance to read it."—*Sunday Afternoon, Springfield (Mass.).*

"We find its descriptions universally good, that it is admirably simple and direct in style, without waste of words or timidity of opinion. The book represents a great deal of patient labor and conscientious study."—*Courant, Hartford (Conn.).*

"Miss Kirkland has composed her 'Short History of France' in the way in which a history for young people ought to be written; that is, she has aimed to present a consecutive and agreeable story, from which the reader can not only learn the names of kings and the succession of events, but can also receive a vivid and permanent impression as to the characters, modes of life, and the spirit of different periods."—*The Nation, New York.*